Lylian

LOST LAND
of the LYTLES

Lylian

LOST LAND
of the LYTLES

BY

THOM SANDBERG

Whizbang Press

718 Washington Avenue North
Minneapolis, Minnesota 55401

This is a work of fiction. All of the characters, organizations, and events portrayed in this novel are either products of the author's imagination or are used fictitiously.

Library of Congress Control Number: 2015916343
Sandberg, Thom
      Lylian, Lost Land of the Lyltes / Thom Sandberg
        p. cm.
      ISBN 978-0-9968873-0-4
      1. Fiction

Designed by Tony Redunzo

For their help with this book, the author, in no particular order and completely understanding he is forgetting many, is grateful to Mary Logue, Maren Hoven Dale, David Housewright, Kathy Mach, R. D. Zimmerman, Colette at Wild Rumpus Bookstore, Drew Daniel Schmalz, Clarissa Hutton, Gail Helland, Rick Dublin, Belinda & Nick Boyd, Cathy Madison, James & Marilee Sandberg, Corky & Em Swartout, Harry & Leslie Adler, Scott Litman, Ray Rybak, Lowell Pickett, Emmett Lamb, and of course, Barbara Kaerwer.

To Martha and Alta; 465

CHAPTER ONE

April 7, 10:45 P.M., Lake Neusiedler, Austria

COUNT JOSEPH EUGENE SAVOY sat in his library, holding a glass of *Kék Bor*, contemplating the future. His years of planning, scheming and waiting were coming to an end.

Sitting next to a roaring fire, he scratched his pet coyote, Justice, behind the ears as it gnawed on a bone. The Count nervously arranged and rearranged a stack of books on his desk, obsessed with making sure everything was in perfect order. The night wind howled with a vengeance off Lake Neusiedler, the massive serpentine lake straddling the border between Hungary and Austria. The Count's castle, Windstorm, sat on the Austrian side.

His estate was mammoth, with stables for 50 horses, forests stocked with wild game, and a retinue of cooks, groundskeepers, scullery maids, gardeners, butlers, and more.

And he hated it all. For the Count longed for only one thing on Earth: to rule the island of Lylian.

He knew everything about Lylian. Its mountains and valleys. The names and street addresses of every shop, store and business on the island. He knew of its extensive system of caves and how one could get almost anywhere underground. He even knew last week's specials at the Café Blue Cat.

Most important, he knew his father had ruled Lylian, almost 40 years ago.

The Count's only problem—he was one of *The Banished*, and could never set foot on the island again. Not that he alone had been banished. His family had been sent away, 38 years earlier. But there was no way back into the island country once a family was forced to leave.

Now he was the leader of those Lylians who had been forced off the island, and he was determined to avenge his family's disgrace.

He sipped his *Kék Bor*, the blue wine of Lylian, and chuckled at the thought that the wine was so hard to steal from the island and sneak into Austria that every sip cost him a thousand dollars. He didn't care. He was rich beyond belief. But all that money couldn't buy him Lylian.

That was about to change. For decades his family had been plotting to retake control of the island. It all started when the Count's father hired scientists to create a disease that—over a few generations—would permanently wipe out a certain sector of the island's population. Sadly, 40 years ago his father's plan was discovered and he was executed and the rest of his family banished. But the virus had already been introduced and could not be stopped. The Count had waited years for what was about to happen in the next few days. Everything had been meticulously planned, every contingency taken into account, and the final stage was under way.

All was in perfect order when just hours ago he learned through his spies on Lylian that a 13-year-old American girl could ruin everything. Somehow she had stumbled onto a possible cure for the disease with some blasted serum she had created. The island was going to make her a very generous offer for it.

"I'll make her a better offer," he said to no one. "And if that doesn't work, I'll simply have her killed."

Chapter Two

April 8, 3:17 P.M., Minneapolis

"This is the worst day of my life," Lucia said to herself walking home from school. "Third place in the science fair. I may as well have not entered."

Lucia had such high hopes for her bee sting serum. But Ethan Oscarson won second place with a stupid robotic arm (okay, it was awesome) and Kathy Johnson (hate her) won first prize with a smartphone app that translates English into a dozen languages. Hate her.

Lucia was something of an inventor. All her life, she had been making things in her family's basement that, to be kind, were simply goofy.

There was the time she tried fitting bird collars for robins, thinking they might make great pets and would be easy to feed. The robins felt otherwise.

Another time she built a fuel converter for the family car so it would run on carrot juice (there being an excessive number of carrots grown that year in the family garden) only for the car to belch orange smoke every time it turned a corner.

A few years ago, she invented a new color, somewhere between purple and orange, that she called porange. For two weeks Lucia wore porange clothes to school to help create a demand for it. The only demand it created came from the principal requesting her to stop wearing that ridiculous color.

Still, she kept at it and even wrote her own Blog, *Lucia Boyd, Girl Genius*. She posted all her inventions there in the hopes of finding a buyer. Still waiting.

And still feeling gloomy from defeat, Lucia reached home. As she walked in, she found her mom and dad sitting at the kitchen table holding a letter and talking quietly.

"Peanut, could you come here?" her dad, Leo, said. "Your mom and I have something rather important to discuss."

Lucia did a quick mental list of what she might be in trouble for but came up blank. Her room was clean, mostly. She was doing well in school, and with the exception of the un-emptied wastebaskets, she was up to date on her chores. Besides, her father used her nickname. He wouldn't have if she were in trouble. Still, she entered the kitchen with a nervous smile.

"Hello, parental units. What's up?" she said, trying to read the letter over her mom's shoulder.

"Well, we received a very curious letter today," Leo said. His voice had a somber tone that surprised Lucia.

Lucia's father was tall and rail thin. He had huge, constantly moving hands; a thick shock of hair that refused combing; and intense but darting eyes that seemed to take in everything but whom he was talking to.

Lucia had inherited the inventing bug from her father. He worked as a substitute instructor at a small college in Minneapolis. Leo knew a little bit about everything, so he could easily talk his way through any class for a day or two. This gave him plenty of time for his own inventing.

Lucia knew what was coming. Dad must have received another

rejection letter for one of his ideas and he and Mom were trying to figure out what to do next. Money was tight, since Dad had put every spare dime into his last invention. She figured there would be no vacation this year. And as far as even thinking about getting a laptop, forget it. Lucia did her best to put a smile on her face.

Lucia grabbed the letter from the table. "Oh, Dad, it doesn't matter what this stupid letter says. They're just a bunch of idiots. I think your idea is great, well, even though I don't really know what it is, but, well, I just know it's great."

Looking at each other , Lucia's parents shook their heads. "Peanut, you've got it all wrong, this isn't about me, it's about you. Someone is interested in your bee sting serum. But you're a minor, only 13. They felt best writing to us."

"Somebody thinks my idea is great?"

"Funny, that's just what they say right here. 'After considered review, we think your idea is just great.' How 'bout that? You finally sold one." Her dad swept Lucia into his arms. "Peanut, you *sold* an idea!"

With that, both her mom and dad started yelling and whooping and pretty much carrying on like crazy people—a recurring behavior in this house—with Lucia joining in. There might be a laptop in her future yet, she thought, as they danced around the kitchen.

After they had so thoroughly hooted and celebrated that they were all quite winded and hoarse, Lucia casually asked—as an afterthought, really—who wanted her serum.

Once again, both her mom and dad got the same weird expression as when she first walked into the room.

"Well, Peanut, the thing of it is," Leo said, "it's a government that's interested, and they want us to send samples to see if your serum can be modified for a special use."

"Yes! Yes! Yes! Yes! Yes!" she screamed jumping on her father once again. Someone wanted something she invented. And a foreign country at that. She could hardly wait to tell her friends. In the excitement of the news she didn't hear exactly what country was interested.

"Dad, what country?"

"Well, here's the amazing thing, Peanut. It's Lylian Island."

Lucia sat very still on her father's lap. Then she came up with the best inspiration of her life.

CHAPTER THREE

April 8, 4:00 P.M., Minneapolis

LYLIAN ISLAND. Leo might as well have called it the moon. Lylian Island was just about as accessible. A place so steeped in mystery, just mentioning its name set people to exclaim wild opinions and offer outlandish speculations.

It's not like Lylian Island was a million miles away or didn't have air to breathe. Lylian had plenty of air and lay about 1,400 miles east of Delaware, smack in the North Atlantic Ocean. The island would be a hop, skip and a jump away from just about anywhere in the U.S.

But no one traveled to Lylian Island. Oh, people wanted to; they just weren't allowed. Not ever. Never.

Lylian Island was certainly small. In fact, it was very tiny indeed, about 220 square miles and allowing absolutely no tourists.

That made it all the more desirable. All the money in the world couldn't get you into the country, although plenty of wealthy people had tried. It was rumored that Bill Gates had promised to give the leader of Lylian Island $50 million for a weekend visit and dinner at the castle. His phone call wasn't even returned.

This made Lucia all the more certain her inspiration was brilliant. She looked at her parents and said in her most determined voice, "Mom, Dad, they can have a sample, but only if I bring it to them."

Her parents stared at her in disbelief.

"Lucia, are you crazy?" her dad exclaimed. "This is Lylian Island we're talking about. Nobody gets to go there. No way will they let a 13-year-old girl visit, regardless of how many bees sting them."

"Dad, just email them—the address is right here in the letter. You always tell me all you have to do is ask. The worst that can happen is you might hear "no." Besides, if they really want my serum, I'm hand delivering it. Dad, think about it, a chance to visit Lylian Island! *Duh!*"

Leo thought about her logic for a moment and then smiled. She was absolutely right. He reached for his laptop to email her request.

The Boyd's had just finished dinner when Leo checked his inbox and read the second most amazing correspondence of the day. In a daze, Leo walked into the kitchen, where Lucia and her mom were finishing up the dishes.

"Ladies, I've just heard back from Lylian," Leo said. He stared at his family in disbelief. "You will not believe this, but they agreed. Peanut, you are going to Lylian Island!"

Lucia stood very still by the sink, holding a wet plate. Then she started to cry with happiness.

The government of Lylian instructed the Boyd's it would allow one adult to chaperone Lucia, and the family decided that Leo would go with her. The first order of business was getting a passport for Lucia. She barely slept a wink, waiting for it to arrive. Without the passport there would be no trip. Lucia busied herself with packing and repacking her bag for the thousandth time and rereading the few books she could find about Lylian. To stay in her parents' good graces, she made sure her room had never been cleaner and she washed the family car every other day.

Finally the passport arrived just a week before their flight. This helped ease her worry, but one step remained.

Her dad had to fly to Hungary.

Lylian Island didn't have an ambassador, an embassy, a consulate or even a P.O. Box anyplace on Earth, except Hungary. All contact with the outside world and Lylian Island came through a small embassy in Budapest. Any travelers to Lylian Island needed to be approved and issued the proper credentials from the Budapest office.

"Youngster, I'll be back in a few days," Leo said, scooping up her new passport and racing out of the house. Jumping into a waiting cab, he headed for the airport.

A moment later, a generic white van with the name "Bob's Dry Cleaning" painted on the side discreetly pulled away from the curb and followed the cab. Leo had no idea he was being tailed.

Returning three days later from Hungary, exhausted, but with the passports stamped and the correct visas affixed, Leo sat with Lucia at the kitchen table and examined them. "Well, I can safely say I've never seen visas like these before," he said.

Glued onto a page in each passport was a heavy sheet of paper with ornate borders printed in green metallic ink that glittered in the sunlight from the kitchen window.

"I don't understand a single word," Lucia said. "But I know this old engraving of a cat with a crow sitting on its back is their official seal. I saw it in a book." Lucia smiled with excitement as the trip became all the more real.

"Dad, what's this?" Lucia asked.

In the lower corner of the page was another, much smaller sheet affixed to it. It was so tiny and hard to read that she got out a magnifying glass from the junk drawer for a closer look. She soon realized it was an exact copy of the larger sheet, only this one appeared in blue metallic ink and there was no crow sitting on top of the cat. Looking even closer, she could see this cat clutched black feathers in its mouth.

Under the engraving, printed in incredibly tiny type, was the message: *"Lylian Island Welcomes Lucia,"* printed in the deepest blue metallic ink she'd ever seen.

Chapter Four

April 20, 10:43 A.M., Minneapolis

Arriving at the airport, Father and Daughter marched excitedly to the international flight desk for Delta Airlines, and it was only then that Lucia fully realized how difficult it was to get to Lylian. Just as her father had to travel to Hungary for the visas, they had to fly there again for a connecting flight to the island. The official Lylian airline, *LylAir,* only offered flights once every other Thursday and only from Budapest.

"Do you have bags to check?" the ticket agent asked.

"These two," Leo said. He hoisted the large bags onto the scale. "Lucia, are you checking your backpack?"

"Checking my backpack? Dad, I'm going to sleep with this puppy. It's got my bee sting serum in it, and it's never going to leave my sight."

They cleared security and were about to sit down and have some ice cream when two men dressed in drab black suits and scuffed shoes came up to them. One was of normal build and wore his thick black hair long and parted down the middle. It glistened with grease. The second was short and stocky with a sparse head of hair and a goatee.

"Mr. Boyd, may we have a word with your daughter?" the stocky one asked. He pulled out his wallet and showed her father a silver U.S. government badge.

"If the two of you will follow us, we will only take up a moment of your time." They smiled, but their eyes meant business.

Following the two government agents down a hall, Lucia and her dad were led into a tiny office the size of a broom closet.

"Impressive office," Lucia said. "Any smaller and you would have to work standing up." She was nervous, but wasn't going to let them know.

The stocky agent ignored Leo and addressed her directly. "Young lady, we understand you are going to Lylian for the sole purpose of selling some sort of invention to their government."

"How do you know that?" Lucia asked.

"Let's just say we have our sources," the agent said. "However, we don't quite know *what* it is. We're here to ask you, on behalf of the United States of America, to tell us."

"Let me see it now," the long-haired agent snarled. He moved closer to Lucia and reached for the backpack, but as he shifted to his feet, Lucia noticed a gun strapped to his side.

She instinctively clutched her backpack and stepped back.

"What governmental agency are you with again?" Leo demanded. The agents looked nervously at each other.

"That's not important right now," the fat agent said.

"Something's not right here," Lucia said. "Sorry, but this conversation is over. Dad, let's go, we've got a plane to catch."

Exiting the room and hurrying toward the gate, Lucia glanced over her shoulder and found the two men had vanished into the crowd.

12

Chapter Five

April 20, 7:35 P.M., Budapest

Lucia felt like a traveling rock star as she stepped out of customs at Budapest's Ferihegy Airport to find someone had hired them a driver, a small man in a black suit, smoking a cigarette and holding a placard with their names on it.

"Dad, how awesome is that?" So far the trip was too good to be true.

The driver wordlessly took their bags and led them through the terminal. Outside, a large black car sat parked at the curb. It was long and old and gleamed like a mirror in the sun. The driver put their bags into the trunk and opened the door for them. Getting into the car, Lucia noticed a small insignia on the door showing a small cat with a crow sitting on its back.

As the car entered Budapest, Lucia and Leo marveled at the architecture and the people walking about.

"Budapest is really two old towns, Buda and Pest, that merged in 1873," Leo said. "We're driving through the Pest side now. Buda is across the Danube River, right by our hotel."

"Sort of like Minneapolis and St. Paul?" Lucia asked. "Think *they'll* ever merge?"

"Yes, about the same time you sprout wings and learn to fly."

The car continued through town, down narrow streets with

13

magnificent old buildings on each side, arriving at the Four Seasons Hotel just as the sun was beginning to set. It bathed the creamy white marble walls as the building glowed with light pouring from all the windows. A Porter helped them out of the car as the driver retrieved the luggage.

A man dressed in a dove-gray morning jacket walked out of the huge entryway to greet them. "*Jo napot kivanok*, good evening. I'm the hotel manager, and you must be Mr. Boyd. It is a pleasure to have you stay with us. Miss Lucia, welcome to Budapest."

The manager quickly checked them in and then escorted them to their third-floor suite. Their corner room gave them a fabulous view of the Danube River and the city below. After the manager left, they unpacked their pajamas for the night.

"Remember, we need to get an early start tomorrow," Leo said. "Let's find a restaurant nearby and then perhaps after dinner we can walk along the Danube."

Lucia grabbed her backpack and the two went down to the lobby. Asking the concierge for a good restaurant in the area, they were directed to the Restaurant Múzeum, a 15-minute walk away. The air felt crisp as they strolled down the narrow cobbled streets, stopping on occasion to window-shop the small stores they passed.

They were so enchanted by the beautiful old city that neither of them noticed a large orange and gray cat following them from the rooftops as they walked to dinner.

The restaurant, located near the National Museum, was small, rustic and busy. They settled into a table in the corner, and after a very long look at the menu, ordered dinner.

"Dad, I want to explore Lylian Island from top to bottom," Lucia said.

"We can sure try, but this is a business trip, and I imagine we'll be in a lot of meetings. That doesn't mean we can't find you a good tour guide to help you see the sights. But business first."

"Dad," she said between bites of goulash. "What do you think they want with my bee sting serum?"

"We'll just have to find out when we meet with them. Finish your goulash and let's head back to the hotel. It's getting late."

Lucia smiled at her dad and decided not to press the issue.

They paid the waiter and walked silently down to the Danube River, a few blocks away.

The cat continued to silently follow behind them, staying to the shadows. The night had cooled but felt good after the warm restaurant and heavy food. Soon they reached the river.

After a moment to appreciate the view they continued on, with Leo talking about Hungary's place in the world economy. As her father spoke, Lucia let her gaze drift over the city and its beautiful lights twinkling around her. Every few minutes she would nod her head and say "hmmm," so her dad would think she was listening.

Looking around, Lucia had thought they were alone until she noticed two figures, one taller than the other, standing in the shadows of the Chain Bridge a little further down the quay. Lucia couldn't quite make them out and would have thought little more about them until one lit a cigarette and the match's glow highlighted his face.

It was the two government agents who questioned them at the Minneapolis airport.

"Dad, Dad, Dad!" she whispered. She tried to remain calm, "Don't look now, but the two guys from the airport are here. They're behind you, under the bridge."

Her dad stood still for a moment and, trying to look natural, started using his hands to point at interesting sights around them. As he gestured at the architecture, he casually turned around so he could see the two figures under the bridge. He continued his random pointing until he had his back to them again.

"Let's head up to the hotel," he said. "And this time, let's not dawdle."

He placed his arm protectively around Lucia's shoulder and marched her up the road.

The agents waited a moment and then followed them. Neither saw the large orange and gray cat silently lunge off the bridge abutment. Pouncing, the cat hit the greasy-haired agent squarely in the back. The force and the surprise sent him into the Danube River with a splash.

Landing on its feet, the cat spun around and attacked the stocky agent, digging its back claws into his corpulent midsection. The agent stumbled and the cat swiped its forepaw across the startled man's face. The man let out a gasp of air, and he, too, fell backward into the river.

Satisfied with his work, the cat ran on, following the father and daughter as they walked safely, but urgently, back to their hotel.

Chapter Six

April 21, 9:10 A.M., Budapest

Lucia had eagerly researched the details of her adventure and knew that Ferihegy Airport had three terminals, the last one for foreign airlines. She assumed it would be their destination. But the driver continued past the last terminal and drove until he came to a small, nondescript building well past the others. The building had no windows, only a small blue door. The driver stopped at the building and, without a word, got out and helped them out of the car.

He indicated they were to enter the blue door and turned to retrieve their bags from the car's trunk. At first Lucia thought this must be some kind of a mistake—that is, until she looked more closely at the entrance and noted the faded image of a cat with a crow sitting on its back.

Soon they stood in a dimly lit room containing a reception desk along with a couple of overstuffed sofas and chairs. After her eyes adjusted to the light, Lucia noticed in the corner of the room two additional sofas and chairs, almost doll size, and her skin got all tingly.

The driver brought in their bags, tipped his head in farewell and left them. They were alone only a few minutes when a tall man walked in holding a folder and headed to the reception desk. He was dressed in blue jeans, a white shirt with huge billowing sleeves, a head bandana, and brown leather boots riding up over his knees and folded back down. He had tattoos around his neck that disappeared under his clothing, and both ears were pierced heavily. No doubt about it, this was a real, native Lylian.

He smiled. "Good morning Mr. Boyd, Miss Boyd. I see you have arrived in Hungary safely."

Lucia felt a little disappointed that he didn't say "Arrrgh," like the pirate he resembled. In fact, his accent was slightly British and very precise.

"Your flight is ready for departure," he said. "There normally aren't many passengers to Lylian. The few other travelers are already seated on the plane. So if you wish, follow me, and we'll get you on your way."

While the Boyds busily gathered their bags, a large orange and gray cat slipped through the door the gate agent held open, brushing against the agent's leg as he left the room.

The Boyds followed the gate agent down a small hallway into a hangar just large enough to hold a Boeing business jet. It was painted dark blue with light blue trim, and on the tail was the unmistakable image of a cat with a crow atop its back.

"This way, please," the gate agent said. "You'll have to excuse this secrecy, but we find it easier to come and go without prying eyes looking at our passengers." He led them over to the gangway and showed them to their seats. The cabin looked like a flying living room with spacious seating for maybe 40 people but Lucia could see only three others. The seats were comfortably padded and covered in light blue leather. Embossed on each backrest was the crest of Lylian.

The gate agent bid them safe travel and left the plane, sealing the cabin shut. The cockpit stood open, and Lucia watched the flight staff preparing for departure. They seem normal enough, she thought to herself, until the captain came out to say hello and she saw he was wearing the same style boots as the gate agent's, only in deep blue with a yellow patch of leather going up each side.

"Good morning and welcome to LylAir," he said. "We are cleared for takeoff, and our flight time should be around eight-and-one-half hours. Please make yourselves comfortable. Your flight attendant today is Singer, and she will be out shortly to explain in-flight safety procedures. Enjoy your flight."

The pilot tipped his hat, returned to the cockpit and sealed it shut.

Lucia and her dad busied themselves getting comfortable and adjusting their seats and the small TV screens that popped up from the armrests. As the hangar opened and the jet taxied out onto the runway, Singer entered from the back of the cabin. The flight attendant was dressed in an ankle-length bright floral skirt that fell over bright pink leather boots. She wore a peasant-style shirt and, over that, a tight-fitting vest. Her large gold hoop earrings; long, thick black hair falling in huge curls; and dozens of colorful tattoos complemented it all. By the nature of her wild appearance, there was no mistaking this flight attendant for anything but another Lylian, Lucia thought.

And it had to be Singer, because, well, she was singing.

She was singing about the seatbelts and singing about the flotation devices. She sang about the emergency oxygen masks that came down from overhead and how you needed to put them on first before helping small children. When she sang that part, she happily sang it in Lucia's direction. Finally, she sang that all carry-on luggage needed to be stowed at this time, and then sat down in her jump seat and buckled herself in.

Lucia looked at Leo and rolled her eyes and then looked down to ensure her backpack was safely in place.

The deep blue jet took off and rose quickly into the clouds blocking any chance of seeing a little of Hungary from the sky.

In the excitement of boarding, Lucia hadn't really checked out the other passengers. The seatbelt sign turned off and Lucia got up to get a couple magazines from the overhead container and casually observe the other travelers. They consisted of an older man, another man who appeared to be in his twenties, and a girl a bit older than Lucia, maybe 15 or 16.

The younger of the two men was dressed in what a punk pirate might wear, all in black. His hair was spiked, and he wore motorcycle boots and black jeans with dozens of safety pins decorating them.

The girl's hair was cut short and dyed bright blue, with white highlights. Her blue suede vest and pants made her appear like a cross between Pocahontas and Peter Pan. By contrast, the older man's attire could have made him one of her dad's business friends, in a charcoal gray suit, white shirt and dark red tie. The ruby earring hanging from his left earlobe was the only odd thing Lucia noticed about him.

The three seemed equally curious about Lucia and made no attempt to hide their gaze. Lucia blushed bright red, smiled in their direction and quickly sat down. The blue-haired girl smiled back at her and then whispered something to the young man sitting beside her.

In Lucia's hurry, one of her magazines fell from her lap into the aisle. Bending down to pick it up, she looked back down the aisle for one more glimpse of her surroundings. She noticed a door toward the tail of the plane, which she thought must lead to the galley. But it was not an ordinary door, for at the bottom of it was a smaller version, like you sometimes see for pets. This one was barely 12 inches tall, and unlike a pet door, it had a handle. And a lock.

———

Lucia dozed after takeoff. After sleeping for almost an hour, she woke, rubbed her eyes and looked around. Nearly everything appeared as before. Her dad was eating a snack and enjoying a glass of wine while reading his book. Singer was singing the lunch options to the girl with blue hair, while the boy sat with his eyes closed, ear buds on, and listened to his smartphone. The only thing different was that the older man no longer wore his conservative charcoal gray suit. He was now decked out in what looked like Chinese pajamas in deep burgundy red with gold and blue dragons embroidered on the arms and across the chest. On his head perched a snug black silk skullcap with a red tassel. All in all, his ruby earring fit this outfit much better than it did the suit, Lucia thought.

Singer came to Lucia and her father next and in her bright voice sang the lunch options. After ordering, Lucia got up to use the restroom in the back of the plane. She passed the three other passengers, and as she did so, the blue-haired girl looked up from the magazine she was reading. Lucia blushed a second time, timidly said hello and ducked into the lavatory to catch her breath.

She was very excited. After all, this was the first Lylian she had ever said hello to, and it was a girl near her age. She took a few extra minutes to comb her hair, wash her face and make herself as presentable as possible. She practiced her smile in the mirror and went out to introduce herself.

"Excuse me, my name is Lucia Boyd. I'm from the United States, and this is my first trip to Lylian. I can hardly wait to get there."

The girl with the blue hair didn't say anything at first but just stared at her. Lucia was about to die of embarrassment when the girl laid her magazine down and slowly said, "Hello, I'm Nikita. This is my brother, Laszlo, and this is my father." Her English was very good, but she spoke with what sounded like an Eastern European accent, not unlike what Lucia had heard in Hungary.

"I take it you are from Lylian?" Lucia asked.

"Yes, and like you, I cannot wait to arrive."

"*Ohmygosh*, you have to tell me everything about it; where should I go, what should I do, what should I see?"

Nikita smiled. "You have so many questions," she said. "I don't know if the plane ride will be long enough to answer them all."

They talked for a few minutes more before Singer came out with the start of lunch.

"Let us finish lunch, and then we may talk some more," Nikita said.

Lucia returned to her seat and told her dad about her new friend. "Dad, I wonder if her father works for the government. Maybe he even works for the king. Imagine, she might even have *met* the king!"

"On Lylian he's not called the king, he's called the captain," Leo corrected.

Lucia stabbed a fork into her salad and ate as fast as she could to hurry lunch along, all the while thinking about Nikita and her almost-certain encounters with the king—or captain—of Lylian. By the end of the meal, Lucia had convinced herself that Nikita would become her new best friend.

After Singer had cleared the plates and served a dessert of sliced fruit with a dark blue cream sauce, Lucia excused herself and went to talk further with Nikita. But Nikita was nowhere in sight. "She must be in the bathroom," Lucia thought. She sat down to wait for her to come out. She waited and waited. The girl never returned to her seat. Lucia then went to find her in the bathroom, but it wasn't occupied.

How odd, she thought. There was only the one, and certainly she couldn't have gone into the cockpit without me seeing her. The only other place she could be was behind the door at the end of the jet, with the smaller one built in.

What—and who—was in there?

Lucia stood there, in deep thought, when it opened and out walked Nikita.

"Hello," Nikita said, "are you ready for our little talk?"

Lucia, peering through the door, could make out a row of tiny leather chairs, scarcely large enough for a doll.

And as Nikita shut the door, Lucia could swear she saw a cat's orange tail.

Chapter Seven

April 21, 11:00 A.M., Over the Atlantic Ocean

The two girls sat a couple of seats away from the other travelers. Nikita's dad was working on his laptop, and Laszlo, eyes still closed, stayed absorbed in his music. Lucia could see her own dad was watching a movie.

"I am beyond excited," Lucia said, "I mean, for anyone who has any spark of an imagination, Lylian is the place to go. I've heard about it since I was a baby. My parents would tell me bedtime stories about Lylian and show me pictures. Not that there are many pictures."

"That outsiders know little is as it should be," Nikita said proudly. "The Captaincy of Lylian is very old—nearly as old as your America—and for some on the island, much, much, much older than that. Now tell me what you know about my country."

"It was discovered by pirates, I think, in the 1500s," said Lucia. "They found some old book in Europe that gave directions to the island and, more important, gave them instructions on how to navigate through the crazy currents, whirlpools and riptides that surround the island. Because they were the only ones skilled enough to land on the island, they could live free of invasion by another country.

"I also know that, because it is so isolated, people from Lylian tend to be a bit ... err... odd. That is, to us, I mean. But I think it's totally wonderful!

"Please excuse me if I insult you — *I really don't mean to* — it's just I've been told how you are all so content to live apart from the rest of the world and that you only leave the island to add to your fortunes. And I've heard you do that by any means you can."

"And finally, I know a few stories about the *Lytles,*" she whispered. "Are they true?"

Nikita gave her a cool look. She ignored her last question and said, "So basically, you are telling me you know nothing."

"Well, I just know what everybody else knows about Lylian," Lucia said defiantly. "After all, it's not like you don't keep the mystery going. Mystery is cool, but you could let out a little information."

Lucia tried to be polite, but at the same time she held her ground.

Nikita looked at her with the same cool expression. Soon it softened into a smile. "I like you, Lucia Boyd," she said. "You are strong of mind, like a Lylian. Let me fill in a few blanks for you. You do have a few of the facts correct, but there is much more to the story. Yes, the island was discovered by a band of pirates and that is why they created a government led by the Supreme Captain and not a king. Even the island's second-highest-elected official, the Navigator, takes his title from our pirate heritage. You see, Lucia, our ancestors were much more than your average ruthless, cutlass-wielding, thieving, murderous, run-of-the-mill pirates. Every time I see a picture of what they supposedly looked like in some American history book, pictured next to that horrible Long John Silver, it makes my blood boil."

As the plane continued across the Atlantic, Nikita relayed the magical history of her island home.

The men and women who founded Lylian were some of the brightest people of their time and banded together from many nations. They were Italian, Greek, French, Arabian, Egyptian, Austrian,

Norse, Croatian Gypsy, German, Chinese and, of course, Hungarian. It was a Hungarian who led them and who first discovered the secret of Lylian Island. His name was Christopher Corvinus, and he was the grandson of the last great king of Hungary, Matthias Hunyadi, who reigned in 1457.

One of the first things the young King Matthias had created was a powerful and noble army for Hungary, called the Black Army. They were fierce warriors, and King Matthias gave them the best horses and weapons. They were respected throughout Europe for their fighting skills and loyalty to their liege.

King Matthias envisioned Hungary as a great nation and employed the best architects and artists from all across Europe to build him beautiful cities. One of the most beautiful and grandest buildings ever constructed in Hungary was his beloved Visegrád Castle. It was there he built a library to house his enormous collection of books. It was one of the largest of the time, second only to the Vatican library.

He lost his throne in part because he trusted an evil man called Vlad the Impaler, the Prince of Wallachia. History remembers him by his other name, Dracula.

"Dracula is part of Lylian's history?" Lucia asked incredulously.

"Why, yes. Matthias and Dracula were to fight the Ottomans in the Battle of Bucharest, and Dracula and his army purposely lost so Matthias would be defeated and his kingdom ruined. Dracula supposedly died in this battle, but his body was never found."

Nikita took a sip of her soda, while Lucia absorbed what she was hearing.

Nikita went on to explain that Matthias' son, János, was never meant to be king. He was not very bright, and his court plotted against him, tricked out of his throne by those he trusted. János lived for the most part in Hungary and married a miserable old shrew named Beatrice, who gave him one son, born in the year 1499 and named Christopher. Beatrice was hardly a model wife and even less a doting mother. She poisoned her husband to gain control of the estate when the boy was only two years old. She had planned to poison the boy as well, once a decent amount of time had elapsed. Two deaths in the family so close together would only point a finger toward her involvement. Unbeknownst to Beatrice, baby Christopher had two very capable protectors, a married couple named Béla and Aliza, who were loyal servants of King Matthias.

Béla and Aliza watched the mother closely, certain she had killed János and would soon do in the boy. The night they witnessed her preparing a poisoned drink for the baby Christopher, they switched it with a deep-sleeping potion that would make the child appear dead. As the mother pretended to be grieving over her deceased boy, Béla found a dead dog in a back alley, and that night they also switched child and dog, burying the latter in place of the child. The next day the two servants packed up their belongings and left with Christopher.

"What happened to Beatrice?" Lucia asked.

"She died from eating a poisoned pear cake that Aliza had kindly left for her before their departure," Nikita said with a smile.

Nikita explained that the three traveled to Visegrád Castle, several days' journey away, to retrieve something very valuable that Matthias had hidden in a secret cache. This would be difficult because one could not simply go up to the front door, knock on it and say, "Hello, I'm here for some hidden treasures." But Béla had been much more than just a servant of Matthias; he had been a trusted friend since childhood. He had been there when the castle's library was constructed and knew there were several ways into the castle besides just the front door. You see, Visegrád sits high on a hill beside the bank of the Danube River. Down at the river's edge, some distance from the castle, was a small cave beside a willow tree. In the cave there was a tunnel almost a mile long that led right into the hidden rooms of the library. He knew that, too.

After Matthias had been dethroned, the whole castle, including the library, had been ransacked and anything of value taken. But none of the thieves, all princes and lords, knew about the hidden room right beneath their feet. Béla wasted no time in locating the secret trapdoor and soon was in. He grabbed a bag of gold coins and loose jewels, several musty documents, and a large book bound in blue leather and stamped with the image of a cat. This book was the most valuable prize. He lugged the cache from the room, resealed the door to hide it from scavengers, and raced back down the tunnel to Aliza and baby Christopher.

They secured the services of three Black Army mercenaries who had fought alongside Matthias, and for the next 15 years they wandered throughout Europe, Northern Africa and the Middle East. The route they traveled was determined by Christopher's educational needs. Wherever they went, Christopher learned from the brightest minds. His teachers knew his true identity and had been friends and fellow scholars of his grandfather, Matthias. They felt honored to help the boy in his studies and taught him well.

From Arabs he learned the art of navigation, Italians the science of architecture. In Spain he learned how to sail the seas, and in France how to wield a sword. Christopher learned the language of every land he visited. The troupe, as a necessity of survival, learned the art of disguise very well and blended in wherever they traveled. To hide the wealth they carried, they traveled as paupers on a religious mission. For the most part, they were left alone. When they were not, Béla and the Black Army mercenaries took quick and permanent care of any troublemakers.

Along the way, the party slowly grew in size. Those who joined were welcome as long as they contributed and showed a willingness to teach and to learn. This was an idyllic time in Christopher's life. With his grandfather's intellect, he absorbed all his lessons. In his travels he saw many different customs, countries and lifestyles, all training for the life that lay ahead. For many, these adventures would have been more than enough, but for young Christopher it was all training for one thing, unlocking the secret of that blue leather-bound book that Béla had retrieved 15 years before, *The Lylian Codex*. This book was more precious than all the gold and jewels they carried. It told of a faraway land of enchantment and safety. For years Christopher and Béla had studied and tried to decipher *The Codex*. Whenever they met someone they could thoroughly trust, they enlisted their help.

Now comes the year 1520 and Christopher Corvinus turns 21. His formal education is over. His band of travelers, now numbering more than 100, have reached Spain, where they are preparing for a sea voyage. Using part of their hidden treasure, they purchase a Portuguese Carrack to sail the ocean.

"What's a Portuguese Carrack?" Lucia asked.

"It's a ship very much like the one that Christopher Columbus used when he went on his famous voyage."

Nikita continued her story.

Despite all their precautions over the many years, the secret of who they were and what they carried was known to others. Christopher's band didn't know that for almost 10 years Juana the Mad, Queen of Spain, had been searching for the *Lylian Codex*. Prior to King Matthias acquiring the *Codex*, it had been in the hands of Spain for over a hundred years, so the queen was well aware of the secrets it held. Always just one step behind them, she was determined to get it back for herself. The Mad Queen devised a surprise attack to capture the book.

Christopher's band was preparing to leave Barcelona when the Mad Queen's cutthroats attacked them. The Black Army swiftly stopped the first assault, but they knew they were not safe. With no time to lose, they made for Lisbon to load up with final provisions and arrange one last meeting before they permanently embarked. There they met with one last scholar who turned out to be one of the most critical, because his insight revealed the final secret of *The Lylian Codex!* With this knowledge secured, they set sail for the West and lands unknown.

They sailed the open sea for 32 days before sighting the turbulent waters off Lylian. With most of the crew seasick and everyone afraid for their life, Christopher and Béla trusted that the secret of *The Codex* would guide them through the dangerous waters and used the charts it held to navigate their position from the stars above. The exhausted crew landed on April 7, 1520, in what is now the island's major city, Corvinus.

Nikita paused for a moment and looked at her brother, who was still listening to his smartphone.

"They had made it, and they were safe. After years of wandering, trial and fear, they had arrived. But, just as they finished unloading the ship, suddenly they were surrounded. And not by Indians, savages or Turks, but something they had never expected."

"Were they surrounded by Lytles?" Lucia screamed. *"Is it true? Do they exist?"*

Nikita smiled and was about to answer when Singer came dancing down the aisle. "Please return to your seat," she sang out. "We are about to land at the Captaincy of Lylian. And please put all trays in their upright and locked position."

Lucia had no choice but to return to her seat and wait until they landed to hear more.

CHAPTER EIGHT

April 21, 12:44 P.M., Hungary

THE TWO MEN RODE SILENTLY IN THE LARGE BLACK MERCEDES as they headed up the M1, the main highway out of Budapest, crossing the border into Austria.

It had been less than 24 hours since they arrived back from Minneapolis, and now they were less than 15 minutes from WindStorm. When they reported in, they knew the Count would not be happy.

The driver turned on the radio, hoping to hear a soccer match, while his stocky companion stared out his window, gently touching the bandage on his cheek.

Near WindStorm, the sun shone high over Lake Neusiedler, and the water sparkled in its light. Count Joseph Eugene Savoy stood by the water's edge on a massive terrace that swept up from the lake's shores to his castle. The wind was blowing, and the Count fastidiously picked away at any tiny bit of dirt that might have landed on him. His faithful companion, Justice, was curled on the ground at his feet, trying to keep warm in the brisk air.

Normally he loved this time of day, but now he ignored the brilliant sun as he looked out across the water through a pair of powerful field glasses. Occasionally he would follow a stork's flight along the shoreline, but primarily he watched the distant shore of Hungary. There really was nothing to see over there. A reed marsh. A small boat with a man fishing for dinner. An occasional fish jumping in the sunlight.

Count Joseph Eugene Savoy obsessed because he knew that barely 100 miles away was Budapest and the Lylian Embassy. "That part of Lylian should be mine as well," he thought. "And one day it shall."

As a butler came down to the terrace, Justice leapt to his feet and snarled at him. The butler eyed the coyote nervously and indicated to the Count that his expected visitors had arrived. The Count handed the binoculars to the servant and strode away from the lake, Justice following at his heels.

The Crusade was ready to be set in motion. Years of careful planning and money wisely spent were about to pay off. And if the visitors executed their role properly, success would be ensured. He hoped the two men would not disappoint him.

It was not wise to disappoint the Count.

He marched through the enormous castle with Justice in tow, his staff scampering out of the way. He found the two men in the great hall sitting on an eighth-century wooden pew. They quickly stood when they saw him arrive.

"Your Excellency, good evening," the stocky one said. He quickly bowed at the waist as best he could. He nervously patted the bandage on his cheek.

The tall one with the greasy hair bowed several times and started sweating profusely. He remained silent.

The Count's pet, sensing fear, began snarling at the two visitors.

"Gentlemen, surely by now you are not uncomfortable around Justice?" The Count snapped his fingers and the yellow-eyed coyote immediately came over and lay at his master's feet. "Now, may I offer you a refreshment after your long journey? Perhaps a glass of wine or maybe an aperitif?" Without turning around he signaled to a servant standing behind him to fetch some drinks. "Let us take our conversation into the library where we can be more comfortable."

The Count left the coyote in the great hall and led the two men down a large corridor lined with suits of armor, ancient tapestries and portraits of ancestors long dead. They arrived at the library and found the drinks waiting for them on a side table, along with a silver tray laden with food.

The Count indicated two chairs. He poured each man a glass of red wine and a blue one for himself. The two men took their wine but thirstily eyed the famous blue vintage.

The Count followed their gaze. "Gentlemen, if you deliver what I am hoping for, I believe I can find a glass or two of *Kék Bor* for you."

The two men looked nervously at each other.

"So tell me, how did it go?" The Count settled into a chair opposite the visitors. "I take it the serum is in the car? I expect the girl and her father are happy with the money?"

The two men looked at each other and then down at the floor.

Finally the stocky one cleared his throat and said, "Your Excellency, it did not quite go as well as we planned." He took a big gulp of wine.

"Explain yourself." The Count said. "The family is poor, and she's just a child. You made my offer of $5 million American dollars for her invention, and she turned it down? *Is she mad?*"

"That's not exactly what happened. We never actually offered the money to her ... you see, Boris ..." he nodded toward the tall man with greasy hair. "Boris thought it was foolish to offer the American girl so much money when we could pretend to be American government agents and trick her into cooperating with us."

Boris drained his glass, mustering the courage to talk. "Excellency, we could have saved the Crusade so much money and perhaps … you might have rewarded us …"

The Count sat motionless in his chair.

Boris continued talking very fast.

"We confronted them at the airport in Minneapolis, pretending to be with their government," he said. "We used real badges. I thought we were very convincing. We planned to appeal to their sense of patriotism. What's more, if she cooperated, we would have the serum at no cost to the Crusade. And it would have worked had she not stormed off."

"We decided to go back to the original plan," the stocky one said. "We followed them to Budapest and were going to offer them the money. We were about to confront them by the Danube, when we were attacked by a Lytle cat."

He pointed at his wound. "That's where I got this."

"A Lytle cat! In Budapest?" The Count instinctively looked out the window toward the distant shore of Hungary and wet his lips.

"After that we knew they were being watched, and we never got a chance to get near them. The next day they left for the island."

"Your Excellency," the stocky man said. He bowed his head. "I am sorry. I have let you down. My allegiance has always been to the Crusade."

Boris sullenly stared at the fireplace quietly muttering to himself. "If not for the girl, I would be rich now," he said.

The Count, hearing this, pulled a small gun from his pocket and shot Boris dead. Looking down, he smiled at the fallen body.

"If not for your idiotic scheme, you would be alive now," he said. Delighted with his aim, the Count shot the stocky man dead as well.

CHAPTER NINE

April 21, 3:17 P.M., Over Lylian

THE PLANE BEGAN ITS DESCENT THROUGH THE CLOUDS, and Lucia could soon make out the tiny shape of Lylian Island on the horizon. *It's really not much more than a bump of land,* she thought to herself as she leaned on her father's shoulder for a better look. He had happily suggested switching seats with her, but she wanted to remain in her aisle seat for a better vantage point to see anyone—or anything—in the back compartment.

As she continued to look out the window, Lucia felt a tug on her sleeve and looked over to see Nikita buckled into the seat opposite her.

"I thought you might like me to describe what we can see from the air," Nikita said.

"Oh yes, absolutely. Thank you. It is *sooo* tiny."

The plane began to descend more quickly now, and soon they could make out the shores of the island.

"We are approaching from the north. You can see the island is like a crescent moon with the pointy ends cut off. It's about 23 American miles long and 12 miles across at the widest point. See the little skinny island lying in the curve of Lylian? Its name is Matthias. That's where my family lives. The two small dots nearby are islands called Béla and Aliza. You can probably figure out why. They're all

35

connected by bridges."

As they got closer to their destination, Lucia could see the island in greater detail.

"That large lake sort of in the middle, that's Matthias Lake, isn't it?" Lucia said.

"Yes, and that tiny lake on the island Matthias is Eensor," Nikita said. "Now look over toward the eastern third of Lylian. See the large mountain surrounded by foothills?"

Lucia looked as the plane banked for a turn. She saw the mountain peeking out of the clouds mysteriously. Lucia knew exactly what that area was.

"That is The Tilt," Nikita solemnly said.

The Tilt, thought Lucia. The supposed home of the Lytles.

The plane turned again and made its final approach to the tiny island's airport.

"We'll be landing at the southern end of the island in the flatlands next to Corvinus," Nikita said. "That's our largest city. The airport is only 15 years old. Before that there was no air travel to the island. You had to arrive by ship."

"*Ugh*. I would never do that in a million years," Lucia said. "I've read all about how hard it is to sail those waters." She pointed out the window to the fierce waves crashing all around the island's shores.

"You are right to fear it, for it is the very thing that protected the island through the centuries from many explorers. If Christopher Corvinus had not had possession of the *Lylian Codex*, he, too, would have perished in the waters."

"What makes it so dangerous and different from everywhere else?" Lucia asked.

"It is too much to explain briefly, but the island foundation is full of holes caused by its formation from volcanic rock. The water rushes through the holes and goes totally out of control."

"The island is like a big block of Swiss cheese?"

"Exactly. Now we're almost home."

The plane passed over Corvinus, and Lucia could make out the tops of the buildings in the city below. The plane continued flying lower and lower, banking for the final descent. Soon the lush green hills of Lylian, with larger mountains off in the distance, were easy to see. They touched down and bounced slightly as the pilot raised the brake flaps to stop the tiny jet.

"Welcome to the Captaincy of Lylian," sang Singer through the intercom. "Please remain seated until the plane has come to a complete stop and the pilot has turned off the seatbelt sign."

Lucia was speechless as the plane taxied up to the gate and stopped. Singer hummed absently to herself as she prepared the exit for arrival.

"Welcome to Lylian, Peanut," Leo said. "I want you to have a great time, but I need you to behave as well."

"Dad, I always behave," she said.

As they walked across the tarmac toward the terminal, Lucia grew a bit disappointed because it seemed so, well, ordinary. The only noticeable difference was that, built into each door she passed, appeared a shorter one (about 12 inches tall) just like on the plane.

There was nothing ordinary about the people working at the terminal, though, Lucia thought. Everyone seemed to be dressed like they were going to a costume party. People wore knee boots of every color and white shirts with billowing sleeves and lace. Over them they wore vests, richly brocaded in an array of patterns and color. Lucia suddenly felt rather plain.

She followed her father through the terminal to customs and immigration. There were two processing agents, one for Lylian nationals and another for visitors. Nikita and her family arrived and went to the agent for Lylian nationals. Lucia saw that Laszlo was still absorbed with his smartphone, while Nikita's father was talking to a customs agent. Lucia waved at Nikita, who simply smiled back.

"Passports, please," the customs agent said. Lucia's father handed them over along with the large visas. The agent looked at the photos carefully and then at Lucia and her dad. He stared at them for quite a while before stamping the large visa and their passports with a red seal. Curiously, he then set both passports briefly under the counter. When he handed them back he smiled and welcomed them to the Captaincy of Lylian.

As they walked to baggage claim, Lucia examined her passport visa and noticed that both portions had been stamped—the large one with its big red stamp and the smaller one now had a very noticeable blue stamp.

Lucia joined Nikita and they waited for their luggage together.

"Thank you so much for the history lesson," she said.

"It was my pleasure." Nikita replied.

"Umm, I was wondering, Nikita, that is, if, well, I really don't know anyone here, and it would be so great if you would show me around if it's not too much trouble."

Nikita stared at her for a considerable time. Lucia was getting the idea that people here liked to stare a lot. Finally Nikita said, "I would like that very much. I will call your hotel tomorrow." With that she grabbed her bag and began walking off to join her family.

"But wait, Nikita. How do you know my hotel's name?"

"That's easy," Nikita said. "There is only one hotel on Lylian Island."

CHAPTER TEN

April 21, 4:00 P.M., Prince of Acadia Airport, Lylian

BAGS IN HAND, LUCIA AND HER DAD STEPPED out of the terminal and into the Captaincy of Lylian. It was a bright afternoon, and she could smell the ocean in the air. They followed the signs indicating ground transportation and were soon walking alongside a small inlet of water.

Parked on the bank was a small boat painted bright blue with yellow trim. It had a tiny deck fore and aft with a cabin between that could hold about two-dozen passengers. Atop this was the wheelhouse, and Lucia could see the captain inside reading a book and smoking a long, thin pipe. He had a bandana tied around his head and large gold rings in his ears. At the stern of the boat was a large paddlewheel painted a darker blue.

"That's our ride," Lucia's father said. He handed their tickets and bags to a porter dressed similarly to the captain and climbed on board.

There were a few other passengers on the boat, and all of them stared at the Boyds for a few minutes and then went back to what they were doing. Lucia noticed that Nikita and her family were not among them.

"In the email, they wrote there are roads here," Leo said. "But the easiest way to get around is by water." He went on to explain that the hilly nature of the island made road construction difficult. "It was just as easy to go by boat through all the many interconnecting streams. And when needed, they built canals to make the connections even easier."

"The roads are made of water!" Lucia marveled.

After a few more minutes passed and two or three more passengers boarded—all staring at the Boyds as they climbed aboard—a deckhand untied the lines so the boat could ease away from the pier. The paddlewheel turned slowly as the boat made its way down a narrow channel just wide enough to allow another boat to pass going in the opposite direction. They went several hundred yards before paddling out into a small river.

They traveled past high banks with trees growing right up to the water's edge. The trees were a lush green, and wildflowers grew in a profusion of color. Every so often a clearing opened near the shore and they could make out the shape of a cottage through the trees.

The boat paddled up this slender river almost three miles until it joined a larger one. On the far bank was the city of Corvinus. The small craft chugged across the river and docked at a pier. Several people disembarked while others got on. By now Lucia was getting used to the staring, and after a few minutes the new passengers ignored them. Soon the boat left the station and headed downstream.

They passed the time taking in the strange city that spread out along the riverbank on their left. This was definitely not Minneapolis.

The buildings weren't very tall—mostly two, three or four stories high—and not very large but packed in very tightly and built using every style of architecture imaginable. One thing they all seemed to have in common was a small ledge marking the second floor. It appeared to be about 12 inches wide, and Lucia thought it might be some sort of rain gutter system.

The variety of architecture was simply amazing. There was a

Normandy-style building that would have been perfectly at home in France. It stood next to a Japanese ryokan, next to a building with turrets, pillars and a steep-gabled roof. On the corner was a small pyramid with window boxes holding marigolds.

Along the banks of the river people were walking, conversing, carrying their shopping or simply looking at the architecture, much like the Boyds. Bicyclists rode along, careful to avoid knocking down any of the pedestrians.

Young children held onto their parents' hands as they tossed rocks in the river and tried to hit the boat. Lucia laughed. Children were the same everywhere, she decided.

After a mile, the boat came to another station. "Let's go Lucia. This is our stop," said Leo. They gathered their luggage and walked up several steps to street level.

They stood on the cobblestone street and got their bearings. The buildings were now larger and more like office and retail stores but just as outlandish in architecture.

"Look for *Kapitány Utca*. That's Captain Street, Lucia. It should be around here somewhere."

Lucia looked around, ignoring the constant scrutiny from the locals. "There it is, Dad, by that building with the large gold dragon carved in wood!"

"Good eye; let's head that way. Our hotel is a few blocks down Captain Street."

"You mean *Kapitány Utca*. Better start talking like a native," she laughed.

They rolled their luggage down the street and window shopped along the way. They passed a store that sold nothing but blue items, even blue chocolates. They passed a vest store that sold what looked

41

like hundreds of different styles and colors of vests. Lucia was already thinking of souvenirs.

At the intersections of the wider streets, the building ledges Lucia noticed earlier arched across and reconnected to another ledge. She thought it a curious piece of design for gutters, since she didn't see how they could possibly carry rainwater away.

"Dad, what's with the connecting arches? Are they gutters?" she asked.

"They could be, but I think they might just be for design's sake," he said.

They walked on and found a shoe store that sold the big leather boots everyone seemed to be wearing, and it took all of her dad's effort to stop Lucia from marching into the store and buying a pair.

On the corner, they stopped to look in the window of another leather goods store that sold leather jackets, belts, hats and capes. And there, tucked in the corner of the window, sat a miniature brown leather saddle with blue stitching that would fit perfectly on the back of a large house cat.

Through the window, Lucia could see the proprietor holding a similar saddle and talking, but there was no one in front of him to talk to, at least no one she could see.

"Come on, Peanut, we're almost there." Reluctantly, Lucia followed her dad down the street.

At the end of the block, they found their hotel, a building with massive columns like Egyptian pillars carved out of lava rock. They entered through two huge bronze doors, with its windows etched in images of cats and the crest of Lylian. Above that was the hotel name, *The Matthias*.

The lobby wasn't grand in size but definitely so in age and

elegance. There were overstuffed sofas and chairs, plants everywhere, and a wall of books. Somewhere in the background you could hear a guitar and violin playing music that sounded like old jazz to Lucia's ears. Several people were seated around the lobby reading or quietly talking.

At the registration desk, Lucia had expected the staff to be dressed in the pirate fashion but found something else entirely. There were two receptionists, both very tall. The woman's saffron-colored sari made her seem as if she had just stepped off the streets of Mumbai. Her blonde hair was styled in a bun and secured with silver chopsticks. The man wore a deep purple Nehru suit, his thick blonde hair in gelled spikes. His neck was ringed with a tattoo of a coiled snake, its head disappearing down his collar. A pair of wraparound sunglasses covered his eyes, despite the time of day. Lucia thought at some time they must have been Paris models.

"Good afternoon, Mr. Boyd. Welcome to The Matthias," the man said. "Your suite is ready. Sign this, please, and Sonja will show you the way."

Suite? Very sweet, Lucia thought.

Lucia watched her father sign the guest registry, a huge parchment book, using a quill pen supplied by Mr. Sunglasses. While Leo was busy talking with hotel staff, Lucia looked back through the book at previous entries. As she reviewed the names and dates, she realized the book was over 200 years old. Yet, for as old as the book was, amazingly few guests checked in. The few names she recognized were some of history's most famous—and infamous—people.

"Yes, this way to your room. My name is Sonja. Please leave your bags; Sven will bring them up shortly." Sonja led them up the grand staircase. The Boyds left their bags for Sven, except for the backpack, which Lucia protectively carried herself.

"Sorry, the hotel is very old," Sonja said. "We have no lift, but there are only three floors. Your suite is on the third floor, but you will find the view is worth the climb."

They walked down a central hallway of wood-planked floors and walls of dark wood hung with old portraits. Lucia noted once again that each door they passed included a similar, built-in version of itself that didn't even reach as high as her knee. Sonja led them to the lone door at the end, with the number 317 painted on it in faded gold leaf.

Inserting a very large iron key, Sonja opened the door. Lucia walked in and drew her breath. The suite was beautiful. It was a mini version of the lobby downstairs. There was a small living room decorated with yellow and blue antique furniture, with two bedrooms opposite each other.

The best part of the suite was the wall of windowed French doors that looked out over a narrow balcony to the most exquisite view of Corvinus. Lucia's eyes passed over a few rooftops and out to the sea beyond. "Dad, the ocean is only a couple blocks away!" she said. She opened one of the doors, letting the salt air waft into the room.

Sven arrived with their bags. "May I suggest the room to the right for you, Mr. Boyd?" he said. "I believe your daughter will like the room to her left."

"Yes, absolutely," Leo said. "Does that work for you, Peanut?"

Lucia stepped into her bedroom. It was a small corner room with windows on two sides that offered her views of the ocean and the city. It had deep blue carpet, a small table in the corner with a chair and ottoman, and a single bed with a pale blue duvet and tons of pillows. A door led to her bathroom, and another opened the closet.

"Oh, thank you. This is perfect," she said. Sven and Sonja smiled as they left the room.

Lucia began unpacking and was about to take a bath when she noticed in the corner of the room—unseen at first—two small, perfectly made beds, barely 12 inches long.

CHAPTER ELEVEN

April 21, 4:50 P.M., Under the Atlantic Ocean

VLADIMIR KORPINSKY HAD BEEN A SUBMARINER in the Russian navy his entire adult life and had sailed under every ocean and sea the world offered. He had successfully landed Russian Special Forces on every continent and in all types of conditions, serving his country with valor, distinction and glory. None of them lined his pockets with rubles.

Now he was sitting 400 feet below surface, 500 miles off the coast of America, all thanks to his former commander and long-time friend, the Admiral. The Admiral had called him months ago with a business proposition he could not turn down—one last run commanding a submarine. The time at sea would be less than a month. And the payment being offered was $2 million dollars. That would buy him a lovely dacha outside of St. Petersburg and more than enough vodka.

Vladimir had immediately said yes to the offer without asking any questions. He assumed his employer was one rogue country trying to land insurgents in another rogue country. He considered where he might be going and figured it would either be East Africa or perhaps Thailand. It might even be the Balkan states fighting over their borders again, he thought, but that would be pretty far-fetched.

And then he was introduced to the Count.

Had the money not been so great, Vladimir would have walked away.

Vladimir had thought the Count was quite mad from their very first meeting in Vienna. The Admiral had arranged for the three of them to meet at a small park along the Danube in the afternoon. The Count first seemed cordial enough, with impeccable manners and a slight fussiness about him. But it was the eyes that gave him away. They were cold and ruthless. Vladimir soon knew this was someone you shouldn't cross.

They had talked idly at first about the demise of the U.S.S.R. and Vladimir's exploits at sea. The Admiral urged him to tell of his great successes with landing troops safely in the roughest of seas.

The Count asked him if he was familiar with the Victor II class submarine. Vladimir replied that he knew it well, having commanded one for eight years. The Count and the Admiral exchanged glances, and the Count nodded his head in approval.

"I believe you are the man I am looking for," the Count said to Vladimir.

"With the right crew, I can go anywhere," Vladimir boasted.

"I will hold you to that, Commander. Now let us gather your bags and I will put you up at WindStorm. I think you will find it to your liking."

The three men had piled into an immense Mercedes limousine for the hour-long ride to WindStorm. The conversation was amicable enough, and in no time the car approached the entrance to WindStorm. Silently the huge iron gates slowly opened. The stonewall surrounding the estate was over 12 feet tall and several feet thick. Covered in vines, it effectively blocked the outside world.

Vladimir had traveled many thousands of miles but always

below water. His experience in the world the Count lived in was very limited. The big Mercedes seemed to drive for miles along a well-manicured road until the car came around a corner, and there loomed an immense castle. Vladimir wondered if perhaps he should have asked for more money.

Attendants already awaited them by the massive oak doors, their arrival phoned ahead by the driver. The Count escorted the two guests into the castle while servants brought in Vladimir's bags and whisked them up to his lodging.

"Admiral, I believe it is time to give our submariner a little more information about our upcoming crusade. Let us toast our forthcoming victory with a glass of a most unusual wine."

He led them to his library, Vladimir open-mouthed at the riches around him. The Count offered them enormous leather chairs by the fire. He ceremoniously brought out a bottle of *Kék Bor* and proceeded to open it, watching the Admiral's delight countered by the blank stare of Vladimir. Pity, thought the Count, he had hoped that the Commander would know what a rare treat this was.

"*Kék Bor*," the Admiral exclaimed. "Excellent."

"I'm afraid I'm not much of a wine connoisseur," said Vladimir. "Is it special?"

"Just the rarest wine on earth," the Admiral said. "It's from Lylian."

Vladimir's instincts from 20 years in the military kicked in, and he wondered whether his prediction of East Africa was a few oceans off.

The Count passed the glasses around and raised his to make a toast. "Gentleman, to the Crusade!" and all three clinked their glasses.

Vladimir tasted the blue wine and marveled at its flavor. Even his limited palette could taste that this was the finest wine in the world.

Whatever the mission was, if it would afford him treasures like this delicious blue wine, he was ready to go the distance.

"Now Vladimir, there has been enough mystery about our mission and your role in it. But tell me, in your own words, what do you think we will require of you?" the Count asked.

Vladimir took a small sip of his wine and looked from the Admiral to the Count. Vladimir was a man who chose his words carefully. "I believe, Count, that with the help of the Admiral here, you have somehow procured a Russian Victor II Class submarine. I believe you wish to use the submarine to transport a group of mercenaries from one place to another. I believe, wherever the landing is, it will be quite formidable. And I believe you want me to command the boat."

The Count clapped his hands in excitement. "Excellent Vladimir, I knew you were the right man for the Crusade," and raised his glass in salute to the submariner.

"Now tell me, Vladimir, where do you think you will be landing?" The Count picked up the bottle of *Kék Bor* to freshen his guests' drinks. While doing so, he glanced from the bottle to Vladimir and back to the bottle again.

Vladimir looked at the bottle and the gleam in the Count's eyes, realizing for the first time the destination and the dark plan unfolding in front of his eyes.

"My God, Count, you can't possibly propose to land a Victor II on the shore of Lylian!" Vladimir exploded. "Are you mad? Have you not seen the waters around that island? In the navy we used those waters to test how much punishment a new submarine could stand."

Vladimir took a healthy sip of the blue wine. "I've tried to sail there, Count. I have firsthand knowledge that it's disaster for any submarine to even attempt landfall. And if you somehow managed to get in, how in the world would you ever get out?"

This is insanity, Vladimir thought, and he wondered how he could extricate himself and still keep the Count's money. He smiled nervously at the Admiral as if to apologize for his outburst.

The Count smiled at Vladimir as if his words held no meaning.

"Vladimir, what you have said is true. For anyone to attempt to storm Lylian is sheer lunacy," the Count said with a knowing smile. "But I am not just anyone."

The Count explained his family's history on the island and, most important, his father's stolen secrets. He told Vladimir of his purchase of the Victor submarine and that the Admiral controlled a docking facility off the coast of Mauritania.

"Which boat did you purchase?" Vladimir inquired.

"The K476," the Admiral informed him.

"I am familiar with that one," Vladimir said.

The Count was pleased with this news and went on to explain the secret training facility also in Mauritania and the capabilities and expertise of his mercenaries.

"They are unstoppable, I can assure you," the Count said, with a maniacal look on his face. Vladimir was familiar with such arrogance and said nothing. Besides, all he had to do was get the forces there and leave. How well they performed was up to them.

Months later, Vladimir would clearly remember and this day, ruing it.

CHAPTER TWELVE

April 21, 6:15 P.M., Corvinus, Lylian

AS LUCIA RELAXED IN THE BATH, her favorite place to think, she reviewed the trip so far and wondered if Nikita would actually give her a call. She had no way to get in touch and didn't even know her last name. She enjoyed the city and the way everyone dressed so extravagantly and yet with so little affectation. Like it was perfectly normal to do that. Well, here she guessed it was.

Lucia got out of the tub and used one of the hotel's huge white towels to dry herself. Stitched on the towel was the hotel's name along the island's crest. Hoping they might be for sale, Lucia sized up the towel as a possible souvenir.

Looking through her clothes for something to wear, she realized there was nothing that wasn't hopelessly out of fashion for Lylian. Giving a small sigh, she selected blue jeans and an orange T-shirt. This will have to do, she thought.

She combed her hair, applied the tiniest amount of lip-gloss and went to join her dad.

Leo was sitting on the balcony with a small tray of appetizers and a glass of blue wine, enjoying the setting sun.

"There you are. I was wondering if you might have drowned," he joked and pulled out a chair for her.

"Very funny. I was just recharging my batteries. What's with the blue wine?"

"Beautiful, isn't it? And tasty. The grapes they use only grow here. There's an orange soda for you in the ice bucket."

Lucia opened the soda and took a few olives from the tray and a bit of bread.

She sat down and looked out over the ocean and the city spreading out around her. The setting sun behind the surrounding buildings made the town glow a warm, reddish orange. She could see the waters crashing into the tall cliffs of Lylian's coast. Beyond that, she could make out the tiny islands of Béla, Aliza and Matthias covered in a mist.

Then, over the rooftops, something caught her eye. She sat up straight and blinked.

"Dad, Dad," she whispered. "Look over there."

Leo's eyes followed the line of her finger and saw nothing. He regarded her quizzically. "Just keep looking," she whispered again. "*Look.*"

He followed her gaze to the gutters and arches they had seen on their walk through the city. Suddenly several large cats came running down the path and then up and across the arch to the other side of the street. They sat spellbound as several more came from the other direction in packs of twos, threes and fours. When two cats came from opposite directions, one would nonchalantly jump over the other and continue on its way.

"Dad, I don't think those are gutters. I think they're roads."

"Cat roads," he said. "Ingenious. Wish I'd thought of it."

"How cool is that? They can go anywhere they want and not be bothered or stepped on!"

"With the size of those cats I would worry more about them stepping on me."

They finished their snack and continued to watch the continually growing number of cats traveling around on their second-story roads, like a feline rush hour. Every now and then Lucia noticed a cat moving quickly, wearing a tiny leather saddle on its back.

By now, the sun had completely set, and the olives, cheese and bread were long gone.

"Dad, I'm still hungry. Let's go eat!"

"Just what I was thinking."

Lucia grabbed a sweater and her backpack—never leaving the serum far from her sight—and they walked down to the lobby. Sonja was quietly talking to Sven and smiled as the two approached the desk.

"Thank you so much for the snack," Mr. Boyd said. "It was delicious."

"I am so glad," Sven smiled. "You enjoyed the *Kék Bor*, the Lylian Blue Wine?"

"It was superb. Now if you could recommend a restaurant in the neighborhood and give us directions to get there, we will be even more in your debt."

This immediately put Sonja and Sven into a heated argument, speaking in Lylianese. They talked emphatically, waving their hands to relay the only native word Lucia understood: "No." Finally they seemed to find common ground, nodded their heads in agreement and turned to their stunned guests.

"Please forgive our ... discussion, but food is very important here. And your first meal must be perfect. My colleague"—Sonja bowing toward Sven—"thinks you may prefer something you are familiar with. Perhaps French, Italian or even British. But I feel you would want to try the food of our country. And on that we had

53

a difference of opinion. But now we are happy. We think you will enjoy the delights of *Café Kék Macska*. In English it's called Café Blue Cat. It's not far and one of my favorites."

Sonja nodded at Sven.

"You will find it three streets down on the right and four up," Sven said. "I will draw you a map."

The Boyds thanked them and walked out of the hotel into the cool night air, enjoying the soft breeze coming up from the ocean. Streetlights lit their way, casting pools of shadow on the narrow streets paved in black and white cobblestones.

"Dad, what are these stones?" Lucia asked.

"The black are lava and the white are coral. I understand the designs change to indicate what part of the town you are in."

Above them and unseen, the large orange and gray cat from Budapest followed them on the catwalk.

Sven's map led them right to *Café Kék Macska*, which sat at the corner of a small square. It was surrounded by buildings all different in design but somehow all fitting together perfectly. In the center of the square was a large fountain with a bronze four-masted ship riding on crested waves of bronze; water shot from its cannons.

There were several other restaurants on the square. Quiet conversation and soft music floated from them through the night air.

Maybe a dozen tables stood outside the café, not half of them full. A waiter recognized the two diners as foreigners and seated them at a patio table that allowed them to see most of the square. He handed them menus written in Lylianese but spoke to them in English—and a bit of French.

"Good evening Mademoiselle, Monsieur," the waiter said. "Welcome to *Café Kék Macska*. My name is Sascha. May I get you something to drink?

"I'd love a glass of *Kék Bor*," Leo said.

"I'll have an orange soda, please," Lucia said.

Sascha was of medium height, thin and dressed like a Russian Cossack, with black baggy pants tucked into knee-high boots, a long red tunic trimmed in gold, and a black furry hat half again as big as his head. Around his waist hung a scabbard and sword. He bowed and left to get their beverages while the two tried to make heads or tails out of the foreign menu.

"Dad, what's a *Bugaci Paraszt Saláta,* and does it come with fries?" Lucia laughed as she tried to read the odd entrees on the menu.

"Peanut, I haven't a clue. I think we're going to be at Sascha's mercy. I hope he likes tourists."

The waiter returned with their drinks and smiled, eyebrows arched in anticipation of their dinner requests.

"Yes, well, the thing of it is, my Lylianese is a little ... umm ... rusty," Leo said. "That is, sort of non-existent, really. Could you recommend something for us? We're visiting."

Sascha's smile continued, unchanged. Lucia thought perhaps he had fallen asleep on his feet with his eyes open, when he suddenly spoke.

"Is this your first visit to the *Café Kék Macska?*" Sascha asked. His eyebrows were now arched so high it appeared they would fly away.

Lucia nodded her head. "To this restaurant, to this square, to this city, to this island and to this part of the world," she laughed. "And we're starving."

The waiter paused for a moment and then whisked up the menus from the table, clicked his heels together and said, *"I will make you a special!"*

With that he marched away, leaving the two guests a little apprehensive but excited.

At a bistro across the square, they could hear a table of revelers lift their voices in song and watched as they all stood and sang in Lylianese and clinked their glasses together. Neighboring tables joined in, and even at other restaurants several diners stood and did the same. At the end of the song, people across the square clapped and the table that first started the song all took theatrical bows, laughing until someone in their group threw bread at them to make them sit down.

Sascha returned with their first course. With dramatic flair he introduced their meals: "For the lady, we've prepared *Gombóc Avec Fennel*, dumplings in a fennel sauce; and for the gentleman I have *Halászlé*, our traditional fish soup. *Bon appetit!*"

The waiter didn't leave but waited for them to try their food, smiling at them almost crazily.

Leo took up his spoon and tucked into the heavy red stock of the thick fish soup. "Very tasty," he said. "My compliments to the chef."

Lucia poked at the tiny dumplings in the light blue sauce and took a tentative taste. Not bad at all, she thought. "This is very nice. Thank you."

The waiter bowed and finally walked away, the smile static, nodding his head.

As they ate, a couple of musicians came to a small stage not far from their table. They picked up a guitar and violin and quietly began playing. The music was jazz, Lucia could hear that, but it also sounded like the music a gypsy would play.

"Dad, what is that music?"

"They're playing the music of Django Reinhardt," Leo answered. "I would recognize that sound anywhere. I read that Django played here in the '30s along with Stéphane Grappelli, who played violin. They were gypsies who loved jazz. Every year in Corvinus they have a festival that honors Django's music."

They finished their first course, and the waiter cleared their plates, brought them more bread and refreshed their drinks. The musicians continued to play as several cats raced through the square one story over their heads.

Sascha appeared with the main course, setting two covered plates in front of them. "And now the *pièce de résistance! Gulyas* for you both."

With flair he lifted the two silver domes covering their plates and revealed their goulash, a heavy beef stew with vegetables. And as before, he stood and smiled, waiting for the first taste.

Both took a bite and gave the waiter two thumbs up.

"I told you, *I make you a special!*" He smiled even wider, if that were possible, as he walked away clapping the domes together like cymbals in time to the lively gypsy jazz.

After the main course, Leo enjoyed a plate of cheese and a cup of coffee while Lucia made a blueberry sorbet disappear. Tables at the other restaurants were now mostly empty. Suddenly there was movement above them and a cry from one of the tables. As they looked up, six cats leapt from the building above onto the square.

A Lytle was astride each cat.

People sitting in the square leapt to their feet, shouting, *"Lytles, vagyunk veled! Lytles, vagyunk veled! Lytles, vagyunk veled!"*

The Lytles paid little attention to the cheers, although several bowed slightly at the waist and one even tipped his large-brimmed hat.

Finally, after years of stories, half-truths, speculation and misinformation, Lucia was face to face with real, live Lytles. She jumped up. She sat down. She jumped up again wide-eyed and screamed for joy.

"Dad, oh Dad, it's true! They're real! *They're real!*" Lucia clutched her father's arm so tightly, he flinched in her grasp.

The Lytles were so tiny, the tallest not more than 10 inches. They were a bit stocky and looked utterly fearless. They donned leather clothes and broad-brimmed hats with feathers hanging in back. Each wore a green sash across the chest with similar insignias, as if coming from the same clan or tribe. Around their waists thick belts held small leather pouches, and each carried a short, thick sword.

Their cats were huge, larger then most beagles. Two were black with white paws, another's coat was striped in silver, blue and gray. Two were Siamese. The last cat was bright orange and gray. And although Lucia didn't know it, this cat had been following her for some time.

The Lytles marched their cats around the square while the diners stood and cheered. Waiters were hurriedly setting full saucers down everywhere, creating a sea of spilled white milk.

Sascha came to present the bill. "What are the people shouting?" Lucia asked.

"They are saying, '*We are with you, we are with you, we are with you,*'" he said. His face was serious for the first time that evening.

Lucia continued to stare in amazement as the Lytles commanded complete control of the evening.

The Lytle entourage rode over to their table, where Lucia and her father sat with their mouths hanging open in wonder. The largest one, astride the orange and gray cat, pounced onto the table beside Lucia and bowed slightly. Summoning up her courage, Lucia pressed her palms together and returned the bow.

"Hello, my name is Lucia Boyd. I'm visiting from America, and I will remember this moment for the rest of my life."

The Lytle stared at the two visitors for some time before speaking.

"Welcome Lucia Boyd," he said. "I am Aranck. And this is Bátor." He spoke in a surprisingly deep voice as he scratched the cat's neck.

Lucia looked him over intently, burning the encounter into her memory and bonding with Aranck as a newborn chick bonds with the first face it sees. Her eyes rested on his sword. Lucia wondered how such a little sword could protect the Lytle.

Sensing her thought, with a flash the Lytle flicked his arm high over his head and forward, like he was throwing a ball, and the sword uncurled—click, click, click—16 of them, until the sword grew to over six feet long. He held it firmly in his grip, and then with a slight flick of the wrist, cut a tiny iridescent blue lily off a nearby plant from the restaurant's patio garden. He flicked it into his lap, carefully placed it in a leather pouch and tossed it to land perfectly on Lucia's lap. *"I make you a special."* Aranck said.

Finished with his demonstration, Aranck raised the sword directly overhead, released a lever on its hilt, and the sword quickly collapsed shut.

"Enjoy your visit." He bowed to Lucia then smiled at Leo. "Perhaps our paths will cross again." He and Bátor pounced off the table to join his group.

Without a word, the small band of Lytles leapt to another table, from there to a blue awning and then to the catwalk. They took off at a quick run and soon disappeared around a corner.

The people in the square cheered and came over to Lucia's table to clap her and Leo on the back and congratulate them in a language she did not understand.

The commotion finally died down and the square started to empty.

"Oh, Dad, even if it ended right now, this would be the best time I've ever had!" Lucia said, staring at the empty space where Aranck

59

had amazed her only moments before.

"It doesn't get any better than that, Peanut," Leo marveled.

The waiter bid the Boyds a pleasant goodnight, but clearly his mood had soured from earlier in the evening. Lucia wondered if perhaps her father had under-tipped—he'd been known to do that— still, she quickly forgot about the waiter's mood and instead replayed the vision of the Lytles over and over in her mind as they walked back to the hotel, still clutching her gift.

As he bussed the tables, Sascha was also lingering over the Lytles' visit to the square.

"We are with you! We are with you! We are with you!" He spat out the words. "Bah. Maybe for some, but that is not true of everyone."

Chapter Thirteen

April 21, 8:50 P.M., Corvinus, Lylian

THE LYTLES MOVED SWIFTLY AND SILENTLY across the city. They crossed the wider streets via arches and jumped directly from building to building over the narrower streets.

"Rowtag, hold up. We need to rest the cats," Aranck said.

"We'll rest at the river's edge," the leader replied.

Riding a white-pawed black cat, Rowtag led them to the northeast edge of Corvinus and stopped at the river.

Corvinus was a city surrounded by water and built along a small ocean bay. As its name implied, the Crescent River wrapped itself, half-moon style, around the city, emptying into the ocean on each side, with the city nestled against the cliff's edge. Along the city's perimeter lay eight drawbridges that, if needed, could be lifted to leave the city impregnable—an island within an island.

The cats had been running for three miles from the time they left the small square, and they welcomed the rest. The riders absently scratched their mounts' ears as Rowtag scanned the bridge to ensure they could cross safely.

He signaled his band to follow him as his cat leapt down from a gabled roof to the top of a porch and from there to the street. Soon Aranck and the others were crossing the bridge. Instead of climbing to the top, they went under the bridge and walked across on the stanchions below.

On the other side of the river it was more rustic, with few buildings along the water's edge, which soon changed to farmland, vineyards and steep mountains.

They climbed up the embankment to an outcropping where they had hidden food and drink for all. Rowtag sat next to Aranck, and the two ate quietly.

"Tell me, Aranck, what was the outside world like?" Rowtag said. "Did you get lost? Are those humans any different than the ones here? Is their land as beautiful as The Tilt?"

"Nowhere is as beautiful as the Tilt," Aranck said. "Yes, it is large, but I did not get lost. And it's true you can ride for days—even weeks—in any direction and never see the ocean."

The other Lytles listened, wide-eyed. None of them had ever traveled off the island. The thought that Aranck had actually visited a continent filled them with wonder. While they felt absolutely no desire to ever leave Lylian, they were curious about life elsewhere. As Aranck described his trip to Budapest, including Bátor's attack there on the two black-suited men, the small group sat motionless, absorbed in the story.

"There is not enough *Kék Bor* in all of Lylian to get me to leave our island home," Rowtag said. The other Lytles enthusiastically nodded in agreement.

"I understand your sentiment, Rowtag," Aranck said. "But perhaps it is time we once again let the whole world know of our existence. After all, there was a time when Lytles lived and roamed the entire planet. Who knows, maybe we wouldn't be facing the extinction we are now."

Changing the subject, Rowtag said, "You and Bátor made quite an impression on the girl at the restaurant. She never saw you on their journey?"

"No, Bátor and I were very careful," Aranck said. "But I was able to observe her. She has a good heart and a strong spirit. I like her. She reminds me of my oldest daughter."

"Do you think she understands how important her visit is to us?" Rowtag asked.

"Not at all," Aranck replied. "But I know how important she is to our families—your children and mine. And I pray she is in time to save their lives."

"To save all our lives," Rowtag said.

To recharge for the last leg home, four of the cats curled up for a quick nap, while one Siamese disappeared into the bushes to watch for intruders. Another hunted field mice for fun.

The moon was high in the night sky when the Lytles set off again, following a narrow path due north almost five miles through the woods. They made good time, stopping occasionally to rest. They marched through wooded countryside, which rose higher and became more rugged.

Soon the land fell away again, and in the distance they could see the shores of what the Lylians called Matthias Lake, a lake almost as large as the city Corvinus. The Lytles called it something else. They called it home.

By now they were far from Corvinus. They rode down to the lake, where they rendezvoused with three more Lytles. Brief words were exchanged, a signal was given, and seven more Lytles emerged from the trees, flick swords in hand, ready to fight in the event of trouble.

They all set to work retrieving a sailboat from a small cave along the shore and pulling it out into the lake proper.

The boat was a two-masted wood schooner, complete with spinnaker, topsails, cannon deck and galley. It was about the size of a small American car. It could hold two-dozen cats, riders and crew.

By now the sun's first rays played across the lake to light their work. They herded the cats aboard and set sail.

They headed due east across the lake to the far shore and The Tilt. The wind was strong at their backs, and they made excellent time.

All the cats fell asleep on the deck, with one exception. Bátor hung his front paws over the side of the boat and heaved his breakfast into the lake. Not all cats enjoy the open water.

Chapter Fourteen

April 22, 9:00 A.M., Corvinus, Lylian

"Dad, I may as well tell you now, I'm never going home," Lucia stated at breakfast. Beside her plate rested the iridescent blue flower from the night before. "I'm having my mail forwarded here."

"Well, I think Mom might be disappointed to hear that," Leo said as he drank a cup of coffee.

"Dad, I'm serious."

"Peanut, eat your breakfast."

"Humph!" she said and dug into her porridge.

Lucia stared out at the ocean and contemplated the day ahead. Then the phone rang. Her father went to answer it.

A few moments later he stepped out to the balcony, "Peanut, it's for you."

"Hello?" she said eagerly into the phone.

"Lucia, hello. This is Nikita. Do you remember, we met on the plane ride?"

"Do I remember?" Lucia blurted. "How in the world could I possibly forget?"

"I was wondering if you would like me to show you around today. I know it is short notice, and you may have other plans, but if not, I am happy to."

"*Yes!* Oh, that would be awesome. Wait, I better ask my dad first." Lucia put the phone down and ran to her dad and told him of Nikita's invitation.

"Dad, please, oh *please, please, please*, can I go with Nikita today?" She fixed her eyes on her dad, using her best pleading expression.

"Of course you can," he said. "In fact, this works out very well, since I have a few meetings of my own set up today. You and I can explore together tomorrow. Hey, you might even qualify as a guide by then."

She hugged him for a microsecond and ran back to the phone.

"When would you like to get together? My day is wide open."

"I will stop by in an hour." Nikita replied. "Is that to your satisfaction?"

"Yes! *Absolutely*. I'll be down in the lobby. Oh, what should I wear? It's not like I have anything that exactly fits in around here. Should I be casual or more dressy?"

"American blue jeans will be fine. I will see you in one hour."

Lucia spent the hour trying on clothes in nervous anticipation of her day. She put on her jeans and then tried every possible combination of clothes before settling on a simple green and white striped T-shirt.

She kissed her father good-bye, grabbed her backpack, promised not to create any international incidents and went downstairs to the lobby.

Lucia said good morning to Sonja, who was busy behind the desk talking on the phone. She settled herself into a large floral chair by the lobby window and watched people walk by in the bright sunshine. She had waited only a few minutes before spotting Nikita down the street.

She wasn't alone; walking next to her, still listening to his smartphone, was Laszlo. He was also still wearing black leather, today looking more like a British rocker and less like a pirate.

Nikita was clothed rather simply by local standards, in blue jeans, a white shirt, red brocade vest and red moccasins. Lucia thought that perhaps Nikita had dressed conservatively to make her feel more at home.

"Good morning, Lucia, it's nice to see you," Nikita said as they entered the lobby. "Are you ready for a tour?"

"Morning, Nikita. Hi Laszlo. I didn't expect to see you."

"My father thought it would be nice for him to come along in case I run out of things to say," said Nikita. Laszlo half nodded at the two girls and tried to make eye contact with Sonja.

Lucia leaned over to Nikita and whispered, "Does he ever actually talk?" The two girls laughed.

Nikita hooked her arm into Lucia's, and the two walked out onto *Kapitány Utca*, Laszlo three paces behind them. They headed down the street toward the river.

"I thought we would start with a boat ride on the Crescent River." Nikita said. "You were on a portion of it when you came here by paddleboat."

They arrived at the pier, and without saying a word, Laszlo paid for three tickets while the girls boarded the waiting boat. Nikita and Lucia sat in the very front row of the boat while Laszlo sat a few rows behind. He draped his arms on the back of the seat, stretched out his long legs and seemed, by anyone's standard, very bored.

They were soon heading upriver, the opposite direction Lucia had traveled the day before.

"I have to tell you what happened last night!" Lucia said. She began describing the previous evening's events to Nikita. "I would have brought the flower to show you, but it is so delicate, I was afraid I might ruin it."

"That is a very great thing to have happened. Tell me, what colors were they wearing?"

"Gosh, let me think. Well, they were all dressed in brown. Oh, and they all wore a green sash across their chests. And it had writing on it but in a strange alphabet."

"Green. They were from the Mek tribe."

As they motored up the Crescent, Laszlo lost in his music, Nikita explained to Lucia, "Meks are one of the 11 Lytle tribes."

As the girls spoke, the craft glided past the city of Corvinus to her right and the rugged countryside of Lylian on her left, with an occasional structure or farm sprouting up on the banks of the river. She listened to her guide, absorbing every word.

"Before I can explain more about them, you must understand more about the land you stand on," Nikita said. "Or in our case, float over. This island is as old as time. Our Earth has had many iterations of life. We know that dinosaurs ruled here millions of years ago. Now is the age of man. But, before that, was the time of the Lytles. They ruled the Earth, and now all that remain of them survive on Lylian.

"A millennium ago, this island was much, much larger. Twice the size of Spain, it was home to many strange, now extinct, species. On the flight here I briefly mentioned to you the nature of the island's volcanic formation. That was not only the cause of its birth but the cause of a massive destruction.

"Lylian was formed at a time when this part of the world was encrusted in ice. When the molten magma burst through the ocean's floor and rose to create land, it melted the ice above. These huge chunks of ice, the size of ocean liners, crashed and plummeted down through the super-hot lava, creating a vast honeycomb of tunnels, chambers and fissures."

Lucia listened, lost in the words, watching the city as the boat passed. Minarets constructed next to obelisks. Farmhouses standing next to Russian *dachas*.

"Thousands of years ago, a minor earthquake occurred in this region," Nikita said. "For most of the world, it would have been just a hiccup. But because of the fragile nature of the island, this earthquake sealed its doom.

"It took only hours for nine-tenths of the island to perish into the ocean. The inhabitants had no clue how fragile their island was. They had no escape plan, because they never thought they would have to leave.

"When the end came, it was very quick. And all-encompassing. It wiped out all the ruling species of this part of the Earth, save for the 11 Lytle tribes. Their land had been miraculously spared. And the Lytles lived here, safe in isolation for thousands of years, until Christopher and my forefathers arrived."

Lucia listened as she watched a flock of seagulls fly over the water, looking for dinner.

"I know the island is named Lylian after the beautiful tiny blue lilies that grow here," Lucia said. "But what did the people who lived here before the Catastrophe call this land?"

"They called it Atlantis."

CHAPTER FIFTEEN

April 22, 11:48 A.M., Corvinus, Lylian

THEY HAD TRAVELED UP THE CRESCENT RIVER, halfway around the city, a distance of about four miles by water.

"Let's stop here for lunch," Nikita suggested as the boat pulled up to a landing on the northern-most point of Corvinus. They left the boat and walked up the black and white stone steps from the river's edge to a narrow street of tightly packed buildings. While the pattern of stones near her hotel had been laid in concentric circles, here they made a herringbone pattern.

Nikita noticed Lucia looking at the stones.

"There are seven neighborhoods in Corvinus," she said. "This one is called Moorland. Your hotel is on the edge of the largest neighborhood, Kapitány."

They walked through a labyrinth of twisted cobblestone streets and alleys until they came to a small restaurant with four small tables outside and only a few more inside. Laszlo spoke to the proprietor, who was dressed in a long robe, sandals and turban. The man bowed to Laszlo, showed them to one of the outdoor tables and passed out menus.

Lucia puzzled over the menu, unsure of whether she even held it right side up. "Well, I'm lost," she said with a laugh and set the menu back down.

"Not to worry." Nikita said. "I will order for us."

The owner returned and took their order. He turned to Lucia and said in broken English, *"I make you a special,"* bowed and walked away.

"That's the third time someone has said to me, *'I'll make you a special.'"* Lucia said. "That's weird."

"But not at all," Nikita replied. "It is a national saying here. But beware, sometimes the special is not so pleasant. If it is a special from someone you have offended, it could get quite ugly."

"Please, Nikita, tell me more about the Lytles. How did you know the one who gave me the flower was a Mek? Because he wore a green sash?"

"Yes. It isn't very difficult to tell what tribe a Lytle is from. The Meks wear a green sash, while the Kemeks wear a red one. The Epps wear clothes of woven cat hair, and so on."

"What was the writing on the sash? Is it their name?"

"No, it bears the names of the 16 lost tribes that perished in the island's sinking thousands of year ago. There used to be 27 Lytle tribes; now all that remain are the 11. The inscription honors and remembers those lost.

"Every year on the island's cliff they hold a remembrance ceremony that marks the day the island fell away. They stand and watch the ocean from sunrise to sunset. Then they gather together for a feast with music, dancing and stories of the time before the eruptions so that no Lytle can ever forget."

The food arrived and Lucia implored Nikita to continue her story. Over lunch Nikita described the period after the Catastrophe and the devastation of the remaining Lytles. Not only had they lost family, friends and loved ones—over two-thirds of their population—but they had also lost the rest of the island community. It was a very special place, and then it was gone.

"The 11 remaining tribes moved to the highlands east of here," Nikita said. "There they thought they would stay safe if more of the island fell into the sea. The one good thing that happened with the demise of the island was that the seas around the island remnants became much, much more turbulent. This created a buffer around the island that protected it from millennia of explorers, including Vikings, Europeans, even Native Americans. The Lytles were safe, secure and cut off from the rest of the world. What knowledge there was of this remarkable island nation fell into folklore, rumors and myth."

"Why is the Lytles' homeland called *The Tilt?*" Lucia asked as the proprietor removed their empty lunch plates.

"That is Hungarian for *The Forbidden*," Nikita replied. "When Christopher and his band of pirates arrived and discovered the little people living here, the visitors were in immediate danger. The intruders were heavily outnumbered, and even they could see that, as small as these strange little people were, they feared nothing."

"This book you mentioned earlier, the one that showed them all how to get here, did it say anything about the Lytles?" Lucia asked.

"Yes it did. And that is what saved the pirates. While it did not say exactly who or what lived on Lylian, it warned of a very fierce and proud race, as old as time, who could not be conquered and must be respected.

"*The Lylian Codex* made no specific mention of anything about the island's inhabitants or its past. Had it done so and the book fallen into the wrong hands, it would have set off a gold rush to find the island. Regardless of how impregnable this island seems, someone would have found a way to land and destroy it for its treasure.

"So when the pirates arrived, they wisely came ashore with

no weapons. *The Codex* had prepared them well for the unlikely encounter. Instead of weapons, they brought gifts. It took the two groups weeks to figure out a way to understand each other. When they finally did, the pirates understood that the land to the east, beginning at the big lake, was forbidden to them."

"Thus *The Tilt!* Hungarian, for *the Forbidden Zone!*" Lucia said triumphantly.

"Yes. Now we must be on our way or we will never see even a portion of my country. Laszlo, make yourself useful and pay the bill."

With that, Nikita grabbed Lucia's arm and walked briskly down the street, toward the river.

CHAPTER SIXTEEN

April 22, 12:15 P.M., The Tilt, Lylian

THE BAND OF MEKS STORED THEIR BOAT in a cave on the eastern shore of Matthias Lake. The Lytles were feeling more relaxed now, safely back home.

The Tilt, encompassing almost one-third of the island, was very mountainous, with its largest peaks rising over 10,000 feet. Here, high in these mountains, were 11 tiny lakes, one for each of the 11 tribes.

Water from the river the Lytles called Fury flowed into Matthias at a maddening rate. This river twisted its way some nine miles through The Tilt, connecting to the smaller rivers and lakes that fed it. The entire system of lakes and rivers constituted the Lytles' main mode of transportation, besides their cats.

The band prepared to make their way up the Fury to the Mek compound. This was not as difficult as one might think, since the Lytles had their very own cable-car system.

In a time before the Great Catastrophe, the Lytles had developed this elaborate system of transportation fueled by waterpower. Following the banks of the many rivers and crisscrossing The Tilt's forests and mountains, they constructed curved half pipes—like gutters—carved into the rock, creating a series of interconnecting highways, tunnels and bridges. These railways were about the size of a typical automobile tire cut in half. They followed the contours of the land and at times tunneled straight through the mountains in pitch-blackness.

The railway carried small wooden cars with two sets of axels, one forward and one aft, with six wheels on each axel curving around the bottom of the car. This allowed the cars to move quickly down the railways. Additional wheels rode under a lip that ran along each inside edge of the gutters so the cable cars could not pop off the railway. The cars were attached to giant loops of thin, flexible metal cable—some, miles long. They ran through the shafts under the railway and through falling water. The water moved the cable, and the cable moved the cable cars at an incredible speed.

With miles and miles of railways connecting The Tilt, the Lytles had a fast, efficient mode of transportation.

The interiors of the cable cars were very ornate. The seats were tiny but well proportioned, each a little throne. They were designed to pivot as the cable cars went up or down steep slopes, so the passenger would always be comfortable. The hinged roofs were intricately carved, with windows installed at the perfect height so Meks could watch the scenery whiz past. Seatless cars transported cats and cargo. Finally, there were cars with no roofs at all for transporting larger items held in place with straps.

The conductor sat in the very front and had the important job of making certain they went as fast as possible yet arrived alive. For Lytles loved speed. With the aid of a clutcher that grabbed the cable, the conductor's challenge was to engage the cable smoothly to avoid lurching yet firmly enough so the cable car took off like a rocket.

To be a conductor took many years of apprenticeship, practice and knowledge. They had to know every inch of the routes they traveled, when to let up on the cable and when to hold on for dear life. If you mismanaged your forward motion, your cable car would slow to a stop before it reached another cable. If that happened to a conductor twice, he lost his license. The system comprised not one cable but hundreds. The skilled conductor needed to know when the cable he was running was about to end so he could release the clutcher and switch to another cable. Some cables ran for almost a mile, while others were only a few hundred feet long.

Simply put, it was the best rollercoaster ride on the planet.

With gear stowed, saddles removed and cats settled, Aranck, Rowtag and the others climbed aboard and took their seats. They talked about the events of the day and prepared for the cable-car ride. No matter how many rides a Lytle had experienced, it was never enough.

Alawa was today's conductor, and she made her last-minute safety check of the cars. She double-checked the straps holding down the cargo to ensure it was securely in place. After checking the wheels and housing, she climbed aboard, lowered the roof and sealed it shut. She took her position in the front, adjusting her flick sword to hang more comfortably.

Alawa gave the signal and engaged the cable clutcher.

The cable cars immediately surged forward, rocking the passengers back in their seats. They squealed with anticipation as the train quickly picked up speed and climbed the first mountain.

Alawa revealed her talent for a fast and smooth ride. She engaged and released over 18 times on the Fury until she came to the small Kep River that joined from the east and flowed north. The Kep flowed to the tiny lake of the Kep tribe.

She released the last cable on the west shore, and the cars rolled across the Kep River on a small bridge. On the other side she connected to cables that brought them through a thick forest. Here the cable tunnels were farther from the water's power, so the speed was slower. Several Lytles got up to check on their cats while others enjoyed a snack.

The Lytles returned to their seats for the final leg home—and the most exciting one. Alawa pulled a cord that raised a lever on the outside of the car that bumped another switch overhead as the cable car ran under it. The gutter ahead swiveled to direct the cable cars to the way home along the Mek River. Alawa immediately engaged the clutcher, and the cars shot up and out as though leaving a cannon.

The ride would be short but very, very fast. Mek Lake was high on the mountain. The water that rolled down the river ran swiftly. To meet the demands of the pace, Alawa skillfully switched cables 19 times in the final, eight-minute ride.

She released the cable, pulled another brake cord, and the cars rolled to a stop. Alawa opened the canopy as the Lytles cheered wildly.

They were home safe at Mek Lake, with the 5,000-member Mek tribe.

CHAPTER SEVENTEEN

April 22, 1:20 P.M., Corvinus, Lylian

NIKITA TOOK LUCIA ON A SLIGHTLY DIFFERENT ROUTE back to the river so she could see more of the city. While waiting for a boat, Lucia asked a question that was bothering her. "Nikita, why are Lylians so secretive? You're telling more than I've ever learned before. Why not share Lylian with the world?"

Nikita understood her curiosity. "You are very nice, Lucia Boyd, and I trust you to be a friend of Lylian. But of the rest of the world, we are not so sure. As the Lytles are small to humans, Lylian is small to other nations. So we have a national saying."

"You mean like a mantra or something?" Lucia asked.

"Yes, I suppose so. It is *'Zurzavar Hoz Ellenség. Confusion to the enemy.'*"

People sitting near overheard her words and repeated, *"Zurzavar Hoz Ellenség"* and pumped their fists.

A boat arrived, this one painted a fire-engine red on the port side and bright orange on the starboard, with black trim and a yellow paddlewheel. They continued on the river for the remaining three-and-a-half-mile journey around the perimeter of Corvinus.

"So, what you are saying is, you don't want anyone to know anything," Lucia said.

"That is exactly true," Nikita replied. "If the outside world knew the magic of this small part of the world, they would come and take it away. They would take the Lytles and put them in what you call a sideshow. Or worse, Disneyland."

"And how come the Lytles are so … little?"

"How come you have blonde hair and blue eyes? How come the grass is green or fish breathe water? That is the way it is. They are small, and we are big. But Lytles and Lylians have worked together in harmony for a very long time."

"Tell me," Nikita said. "What was the reception the Lytles received when they stopped at your table last night?"

"People were beside themselves with excitement," Lucia said. "It was as if Lylians were as happy to see the Lytles as me."

"And they were, Lucia. The Lytles keep very much to themselves. And so every sighting is a time for celebration."

"What is The Tilt like?"

"I have never gone there," Nikita said. "It is The Tilt. It is forbidden. Humans are simply not welcome. And we respect that."

"Well," Lucia ventured, "what if someone didn't respect them, or you took a wrong turn and ended up in The Tilt by accident or something?"

"There are no accidents in entering The Tilt. It is well marked," Nikita said, "and if you were to end up in their territory, you would be hunted."

"Hunted? But they are so little and cute. I wanted to pick them up and give them each a hug." As the words came out, Lucia already knew she'd underestimated the Lytles.

"Lucia, if you try and pick up a Lytle it will be the last thing you ever do. They are tiny and they seem vulnerable, but they are fast and cunning beyond your imagination. They fear nothing. And their cats are equally strong. You may think the natural order of things would be for the cats to make the Lytles their lunch. But that is not the case. There is a special bond between a Lytle and its cat. They are family, and each would die for the other."

"Do they come into town often?" Lucia asked, moving into lighter territory.

"Not really. They trade the things they make for products and services they want from us. For instance, they love the quality of our leather goods, so several shops specialize in leather cat saddles for the Lytles."

"I passed a store like that yesterday, and I swear there was a Lytle in the store. Please, more about The Tilt."

The boat paddled down river, leaving the Moorland section of town and entering the Valhalla neighborhood. Nikita continued her story.

"Remember when I told you Lylian once was home to 27 Lytle tribes? There is a rumor even more tribes lived away from the island. If you think about it, Ireland is an easy sail with favorable winds. But all of that is history so ancient, no records exist.

"The Tilt comprises mostly foothills and mountains. The Lytles love water and prefer to live by lakes." Nikita said. "The lakes all feed into an interconnecting system of small mountain rivers. And from this they derive a transportation network that allows them to move quickly and easily throughout The Tilt."

"I wish I could visit there," Lucia said. "To be this close to them and not be able to see where they live ..."

"You must put that thought out of your head," Nikita replied. "Simply do as we do and accept that it is not going to happen. And you are privileged to even be here."

"I know, I know. Believe me, I am not complaining. And you are being so nice—I am so lucky you were on that plane."

"It is my pleasure. I do not often get to share my country with someone. So now tell me about your life. Do you have a boyfriend, for instance?"

Lucia firmly said "no boyfriend" and then went on to describe life in Minneapolis, her mom, her friends and her day-to-day life that seemed so completely boring compared with the wonder of Lylian.

"You are lucky to know your mother, Lucia. Mine died when I was very young."

"I can tell your mother would have been very proud of you," Lucia said.

By now the boat had chugged almost completely around the city and was nearing the river's exit into the ocean. The water moved very fast here and the captain had to manage the boat carefully.

"The Mek used his sword to cut you the flower?" Nikita asked.

"Yes! His name is Aranck. Oh, and his cat's name is Bátor. It was the most amazing thing. My dad and I talked about it all the way home. The Lytle—I mean, Aranck, the Mek — was so tiny and looked so harmless and then suddenly he snapped his arm outward and his sword just exploded. It was longer than I am tall."

"It is a flick sword," Nikita explained. "On Lylian it has a nickname, *The Hummingbird*, because it is so light and so fast, but unlike the hummingbird, very deadly."

"He cut the flower easily enough, but the sword looked so fragile," Lucia said. "How could anything that small be dangerous?"

"Do not be deceived by its size. The arcane technology that made the metal is very old and known only to the Lytles. It is the lightest, strongest metal known to man but has the strength to cut through a tree limb.

"It takes years for a Lytle to master one, and it's nearly impossible for non-Lytles. Flick swords are so light and the flick so difficult to accomplish that they're useless to most humans. It's like flicking tinfoil. Most are from eight to 16 sections long with a mechanism in the hilt that can lock the sword at whatever length is desired. By releasing and relocking, a Lytle can rapidly lock it at different lengths. So in the hands of a skilled swordsman, the weapon is extremely dangerous. Our forefathers were lucky they chose not to fight them. They were battle-hardened pirates, but no match for a flick sword."

"Have you seen one in action?" Lucia asked.

"Not action like in a fight, but I have seen them used. The Lytles have contests of skill with their swords. And each year at the Cat Festival, they demonstrate them in mock sword fights. It's very exciting."

"Cat Festival? What's that?" Lucia said, interest at full pique.

"It's more than a festival—it's our national holiday. On that day, all the islanders come together to celebrate the bond of friendship and trust between Lylians and Lytles. It's called the Cat Festival, because both value cats. The entire island celebrates with huge feasts, singing and a Cat Festival parade. Corvinus hosts the largest parade, of course, but every town on the island has one as well."

"When?"

"It's in two days. You can see a flick sword demonstration yourself. Your timing for visiting Lylian is very fortunate."

Lucia watched the captain maneuver the boat. The boat's giant paddle was now working very hard, not to propel the boat forward but to stop it from being swept out to sea by the increasing current. Yet soon he had the boat safe and secured to the pier.

Lucia disembarked with the other passengers. Here she could fully appreciate how the river had gradually cut a very deep gorge into the land, and the dramatic way the city loomed so high up the embankment. She joined the others and climbing up the several hundred steep steps it took to reach the city streets. There was a small wrought-iron caged elevator for those who chose not to climb, but no passengers bothered to take it, so neither did she. The islanders must look at the steps as a challenge, she thought.

By the time they reached street level the sun was beginning to set, and Lucia was completely winded.

"That's a climb I wouldn't want to do every day," she panted.

Even Nikita was breathing deeply. "Now you know why this neighborhood is called The Cliffs. Come, we can rest up ahead and watch the ocean."

Lucia followed Nikita down several curving alleys, with Laszlo taking up the rear. Once again Lucia noticed the alley stones lay in a different pattern. They were still black and white, but set in long, undulating curves that made them look like ocean waves. Up ahead, a pale blue sky met the end of the path.

They emerged from between two unpredictably paired buildings —one that resembled a Chinese pagoda and the other an English country estate—and strolled onto a narrow strip of parkland that ran along the shore for miles, the entire length of the city. The winding park comprised many different gardens, orchards and topiary displays with benches and picnic spots. There was a small outdoor café where Nikita led them to a table.

Beyond the park was the ocean, crashing into the cliffs below, and the tiny island of Béla less than a mile away. Just beyond Béla lay the slender serpentine island, Matthias. Connecting Béla to Lylian was a long, deep blue cable bridge with a lane for cars and bicycles in each direction.

A waiter came and took their order. A refreshing breeze coming off the ocean helped cool them down from the steep climb. The setting sun cast light on the water and made shadows over their table.

Lucia stared at the water as the waves crashed insistently below. Further out she could see huge whirlpools the size of office buildings appear and then disappear, only to form again almost immediately a hundred yards away. In some areas the seas would be dead calm and then suddenly break into 50-foot swells. Its turbulent, relentless mass was scary.

"How could *anyone* ever sail through those waters?" she asked.

"I have told you Lucia, *The Lylian Codex* is the answer," Nikita said. "The strange currents, waves and whirlpools kept out the small ships, and the dangerous shoals and rocky sea bottom kept out the larger ships."

"Nikita, this is the *21st century*. Don't you think if someone wanted to get here they could? I mean, America and Russia and England—all of them—build stealth this and secret that. How could you stop them?"

"We have not relied on geography alone to protect us. Over the years we have become very good at gathering information on other governments, people and events that we can use to persuade potential enemies to leave us alone."

"Ohmygosh, you blackmail them!" Lucia twisted her head around to see if anyone was listening.

"Let me say that we simply ask them to leave us alone. And they generally do."

Laszlo silently paid the bill while the girls walked along the shoreline. Lucia gathered her nerve and peered over the railing straight down the cliff to the tumultuous seas far below and quickly backed away. As they continued, the streetlights came on in Corvinus, Béla

Island and distant Matthias.

"Nikita, can we see your house from here?" Lucia asked.

"No, it is on the other side of the island."

As the lights twinkled and she took in the view, Lucia realized that they cast a predominantly blue glow.

"That is so beautiful," she said. "There's been so much to take in since I arrived that I never noticed all the blue lights."

"It is our lucky color," Nikita said.

"How can one color be luckier than another?"

"When Christopher landed here and first met the Lytles, he did not bring weapons onto the island. *The Codex* had instructed them to go unarmed, and they obeyed. For that the crew was wise. But when they came ashore, Aliza was carrying a large lighted lantern made of blue glass, which delighted the Lytles and helped greatly diffuse the potentially catastrophic meeting. For that the founders of our country were very, very lucky."

"A color *can* be lucky!" Lucia laughed.

They walked almost two and a half miles along the water and then turned up a street and back into the city. Lucia noticed the pavers had changed design again, this time to a pyramid pattern. The buildings were still a hodge-podge of styles, but now a number of pyramids and papyrus-style columns lined the streets. Occasionally a small square or fountain would feature a cryptic obelisk or carved lion in the center.

"Let me guess," Lucia said. "This neighborhood is called *Cairo*."

"You are close. It's called *Osiris*," Nikita said.

They walked back toward Lucia's hotel, stopping on occasion to window shop or listen to a street musician. The performers were different than at home, Lucia thought to herself. Back there they usually played for money, and here she noticed they simply played for the joy of it.

Occasionally they would pass someone who knew Nikita and Laszlo and exchange greetings. Those they met treated the brother and sister rather formally, bowing slightly as they said hello. Lucia figured they didn't know them that well and were being polite.

It had been a long day, and Lucia couldn't stifle a yawn as they neared her hotel. She knew they must be close, because the pavers were now in the circular pattern she knew symbolized the neighborhood Kapitány. Figuring this out made her rather proud.

"Lucia, I see you are tired," Nikita said. "But there is one more stop I would like to make. Do you mind?"

"Oh, I'm not tired at all," Lucia said. "Well, maybe a tiny bit, but really, I never want this day to end. Where to, next?"

"There is a store up here I want you to see. It is my favorite place to buy boots," she informed Lucia, now returning to full steam.

They turned a corner, and there stood the shoe store Lucia and her father had passed the day before. The shop windows glowed from within as they stopped to look before entering.

The little bell on the door rang to announce their visit as they crossed the threshold. The store was not terribly large but sold boots in every color, length and style you could imagine. There were embossed boots and ones stitched with designs. Some were not much more than regular cowboy boot height, while others came up way over the knee and then folded back on themselves. The folding pairs frequently were lined in bright silk or satin, others with just the simple leather showing.

A clerk came out from a small room behind the counter. He wore deep red boots that rolled down at the top and were lined with a green paisley patterned fabric. He wore them over blue jeans, and on his top half he sported the big white shirt—sleeves rolled up—that Lucia was noticing everywhere. His vest was cut from the same fabric that lined his boots. If that weren't enough, a tangle of colorful tattoos covered his arms, while the long goatee and huge moustache surrounding his mouth could not begin to cover his broad, toothy smile.

He bowed at the waist slightly and spoke to Nikita and Laszlo like he was an old friend. Nikita said something to him and he turned to notice Lucia for the first time. He stared at her and didn't say a word. Lucia could feel her face turning cherry red. Finally, he came forward and grabbed her arm and shook her hand profusely, all the time talking to her in Lylianese.

"He says he is very glad to have you visit Lylian and visit his store," Nikita said. "This is the finest boot store on all the island, Lucia, and I think you should own a pair."

Lucia looked around wide-eyed at the beautiful footwear. She saw a beautiful pair of burgundy-colored boots nearby and casually glanced at the price tag, which was in forints, the local currency. She did the math to convert the figure into dollars and let out a gasp. At these prices, she didn't have enough money with her to buy shoelaces.

"Um, thanks, Nikita, but I think I might want to look around more before I buy anything," Lucia said, trying not to sound as sad as she had suddenly become.

"Lucia I didn't bring you here for *you* to buy a pair of boots. I brought you here so *Laszlo and I* could buy you a pair of boots. It is our gift to you. *I make you a special!*"

"Oh Nikita, Laszlo, I couldn't. These are so expensive. That would be way too generous. You have already done so much for me today. I should be buying *you* a pair of boots."

"Nonsense, it is our pleasure. Besides, I'll get my dad to pay.

Now what is your pleasure? But we must hurry, my friend wants to close his store soon, and I imagine your father must be getting very anxious."

Lucia looked all around her. She tried on the burgundy boots with gold liners. She tried on a pair of distressed black ones that Laszlo nodded at in approval. She tried on long ones and short ones and every height in between. Finally, with Nikita's expert assistance, she settled on a pair of over-the-knee navy blue suede with a four-inch roll-over lined in smooth-finish navy blue leather. They had a slight heel and were the most comfortable boots she had ever worn.

Lucia twirled in front of the full-length mirror to see them from every angle. She hugged Nikita, Laszlo and even the shop owner. "This is the coolest gift I have ever received!" she exclaimed.

"Come Lucia, we must be going. Laszlo, pay and let's be on our way."

The proprietor thanked Nikita and Laszlo in Lylianese. As they left the store, he shouted out to Lucia in broken English, *"Goo-by, goo-by gorl, tank yu much much!"*

Lucia tried catching her reflection in every window they passed on the few blocks back to the hotel.

They entered the lobby and Lucia spied Sonja behind the reception desk and went over to show off her new boots. She had just spun around for Sonja to see better from behind when she noticed her dad sitting by a large palm tree, having a glass of *Kék Bor* with Nikita's father.

They were both leaning forward talking in low voices very intently. Leo sat with a furrowed brow, not appearing to enjoy the conversation. Nikita and Laszlo remained by the entrance, allowing the men to continue in private.

Lucia said good-bye to Sonja and walked over to her dad.

"Hey, Dad!" she said. She came up behind his chair and hugged him from behind. "I've had the most amazing day. And check this out!" She stepped around in front of Leo and showed off her gift.

Leo adjusted his attitude and looked at his daughter.

"Lucia, they look very nice," he said. "But do you have any money left?"

"Dad, they were a gift from Nikita and Laszlo. I tried to refuse, *I really did*, but they insisted. Oh, and it's a gift from you too, sir." Lucia bowed to Nikita's father. "Thank you so much. This is the nicest gift I have ever received." Lucia noticed her dad grimace. "Oh Dad, I mean you and Mom give me great things, too, it's just, I mean, oh, you know what I mean."

"You are most welcome, young lady," Nikita's father said. "I told her to make you a special."

89

CHAPTER EIGHTEEN

April 22, 5:30 P.M., The Tilt, Lylian

THE MEK CLAN BUSIED THEMSELVES with preparations for the Cat Festival just two days away. The Lytles took this day very seriously and looked forward to it every year, preparing with great attention to detail.

The cats were brushed and then brushed again, removing loose fur. Saddles were cleaned and polished so the leather glowed in satiny smoothness. Near the edge of the woods, younger Meks hunted for wildflowers and leaves they could weave into garlands and sashes for themselves and their cats to wear in the parade.

In a clearing by the lake's shore, a group of Meks practiced their swordplay. Rowtag was a master swordsman and along with his wife, Chepi, conducted a class by the water's edge. As he walked through the ranks of students, he corrected their stance and form. He shouted to the students.

"Watch us and learn. You must act as one."

Chepi and Rowtag joined five other Meks to practice their defense forms. They gathered into a loose circle with their backs to the center. Each Mek stood with legs spaced slightly wide, arms resting at their sides. The seven team members looked straight ahead, neither seeing nor acknowledging the swordsmen beside them, waiting for a signal.

The students quietly watched with wide eyes.

Chepi shouted a command and the group moved in perfect unison, their right arms reaching across their bodies and unsheathing the swords hanging on their left hips. Their tiny arms flew straight out and with a well-practiced flick extended the swords to their full length of over six feet. They moved like a well-tuned machine, lunging forward three times, re-flicking and casting the sword outward each time. On the fourth lunge, they let out a deep scream then stepped, quickly flicking the sword to knife length, and slashed 45 degrees to their right.

They flicked their swords again, projecting them to saber length and slashed to the left and up. The seven started moving counter-clockwise, each one now casting their flick swords to different lengths depending on where they stood in the circle. As they moved, the swords sounded like tiny machine guns as they ratcheted to various lengths with amazing speed.

Now the group appeared to break ranks as they ran through the center of their circle, confusing the enemy, only to reemerge on the other side, swords extended to their longest length again and forming a perfect perimeter defense.

They continued their practice, demonstrating speed and dexterity. They all gave a final lunge and threw their fully extended swords high into the air, where they folded up in a flash and came down, like a missile, to land in the scabbard of each Lytle. They stood at attention for a moment, then bowed.

"Now do it like that," Chepi said, addressing the students.

In a paddock near the woods, others practiced a different sport—cat riding.

Within the large enclosure were various obstacles for the cat and rider to jump over, through or under. Event judges had also installed around the paddock narrow beams of wood set at different heights—some only a foot or two off the ground, others several stories high.

There were cats everywhere. Some sat on the fence and cleaned themselves. Others slept under the shade of nearby trees. Yet others were being saddled or fitted with other tack. A dozen more had riders mounted on their backs practicing various skills.

Nosh, the Mek's finest rider, stood a few feet behind a calico cat with white paws and ears. The cat stood still on all fours, looking back at Nosh and purring, its tail motionless. Nosh adjusted his hat tighter and sprinted toward the cat. In one quick motion he jumped over the tail and across the cat's back, landing firmly in the saddle. He grabbed the reins, and the calico took off like a rocket. They ran the length of the paddock to the fence and stopped dead, spun around and bolted back to the other side. After several repetitions the change in direction became even more fluid. Nosh dismounted the calico and reached into his shirt for a cat treat. He led the cat over to the barn to remove the saddle and brush him down.

He returned with a Persian and motioned her to sit on her haunches. Her tail swished back and forth lazily. Nosh let out a war cry and ran toward the Persian. With a bounding leap he jumped through the air to land squarely in the saddle. The cat leapt up, rearing its forepaws in a mighty display of strength as it stood on its hind legs. Nosh unsheathed his flick sword and the two bolted across the paddock toward a barrier. With a mighty jump the cat flew into the air to a high beam and, though the beam was only inches wide, ran its length at full bore. At the end of that beam was another one going a different direction several feet higher. They leapt directly to it without reducing their speed and continued the fast pace. Along the beam they cleared a dozen more obstacles without breaking stride.

Nosh continued his display of skill by climbing, jumping and diving over many different heights. He and his Persian would be 30 feet in the air and then suddenly down at ground level. Nosh climbed by leaps and bounds, and with sword drawn, plunged from the sky with a yelp from both him and his fearless cat.

Pleased with their workout, Nosh removed the saddle from the Persian, praising him the whole time.

Finally, three Meks, including Aranck, prepared to race each other up a tree. They sat at the base of a large round ash; the lower limbs had long ago been removed to make the race up the tree more difficult. Thirty feet up in the tree were three blue medallions. The first one up the tree to grab his medallion and get it back to the ground won.

They mounted their cats for the climb. A Mek standing to one side raised his flick sword like one would a checkered race flag as the climbers readied themselves. The sword came down, and the riders were off.

They raced up the tree so close together it could be anyone's race. Claws ripped into the bark as the riders shouted their mounts on. Aranck, atop Bátor, started to move ahead of the other two. The medallions hung only a few feet away as he dug his heels into the stirrups for support. The cats were panting hard but not stopping.

He reached out and grabbed a blue medallion from the peg on the tree and flung its looped ribbon around his neck. The other two Meks were only a few paces behind him as Aranck turned Bátor and started the more treacherous climb back down. Rearing back in the saddle, feet firmly in the stirrups, they flew down the tree, in nothing more than a controlled freefall.

As they neared the base, with a large growl Bátor jumped from the tree and landed on the ground on all fours. Aranck dismounted.

Bátor, having won the race, sauntered over to a shaded area, sat down and immediately began licking his fur in a show of nonchalance.

Meks nearby cheered and the other contestants clapped Aranck on his back as he proudly showed off his blue medallion.

"It's good to see our trip off the island hasn't affected our skills," Aranck said to Bátor.

Chapter Nineteen

April 22, 8:15 P.M., Corvinus, Lylian

"Dad, I am bone tired," Lucia said. "Do you mind if we order room service and go to bed early?"

"That works for me," Leo said.

Soon dinner arrived. Between huge shovels of food Lucia filled her dad in on the events of the day.

"The city is so *beautiful,* Dad," she said. "The ocean is unbelievable."

She described the boat ride and the narrow streets, the architecture and lunch. Her dad listened and asked a few questions, but mostly let her talk. Lucia liked being able to tell her dad stuff he didn't know, because usually it seemed like he knew everything.

"Dad how was *your* day? You haven't said two words about it. Did you get your work done? And what was Nikita's dad doing here? Did he come to get them or to see you?" Lucia suddenly realized she was missing some important information.

Leo played with the spoon in his coffee cup.

"Well, I had an equally busy day, but not nearly as fun as yours. I'm still working with the government here to figure out why they want your bee serum. They're being so evasive. As it turns out, Nikita's dad works for the government here. He was kind enough to bring me back to the hotel from our meeting on Matthias Island."

"Matthias? I saw it from the park where we stopped for a soda."
Lucia went on to explain the significance of the blue lights and how
a color can be lucky. "What is it like over there?"

For the first time during the trip, Lucia felt a pang of jealousy
that her dad had seen something she hadn't.

"Well, it's hilly, I can tell you that much," Leo said. "And thank
goodness we had a good car because the roads are pretty steep. It
sounds a lot like your climb into town from the river. Matthias
consists of mostly government buildings, but there are many houses
tucked into the hillsides. By the way, I learned the Captain's residence
is on Matthias."

"Wait. Nikita lives on Matthias, too. Just what does her dad do
for the government?"

"He's some sort of liaison," Leo said. "You know these Lylians,
they simply don't tell you everything."

"People sure treated Nikita and Laszlo with a lot of respect. I'm
going to ask her about it when we get together again. The Cat Festival
is the day after tomorrow, and Nikita promised to show me, I mean
us, around. It's like their Fourth of July."

"The whole island shuts down for the festival, so I won't be able
to get any work done anyhow. And I like cats."

"And I like sleep," Lucia yawned.

"Go to sleep, Peanut, I'm going to read for a bit. Tomorrow the
hotel is lending us a couple of bicycles, and I thought we could get
out of town and enjoy the countryside."

Agreeing that it sounded like a great idea, Lucia kissed her dad
goodnight. She had little trouble falling asleep.

CHAPTER TWENTY

April 23, 7:45 A.M., Corvinus, Lylian

LUCIA WAS FINISHING BREAKFAST in the hotel lobby and mentally gearing up for today's bike ride. While most travel on Lylian was done by water, there were a few roads on the island that carried cars, trucks, bicyclists, even the occasional motorcycle. Lucia watched her dad query Sonja and Sven for suggestions about the best routes. This caused a rapid-fire conversation in Lylianese between the two hotel employees, one pointing one direction and the other another. After 10 minutes of discussion, they agreed on a destination.

"Well, my colleague and I think you might enjoy a ride through the countryside to see one of our lovely lakes and then to a little fishing village on the northwest coast," Sonja said.

"The lake will be the most pleasant highlight," Sven added.

"You will love the village," Sonja said. "Come let me show you on your map."

With directions in hand, Lucia and her dad found their bikes.

"Boy, Sonja and Sven sure like to argue with each other," Lucia said.

"I wonder if they're married," Leo said.

Lucia adjusted her backpack and they set off down the street. "Dad, where are we headed, and how many miles are we riding?"

"We're going to bike north and west of here. All in all, maybe 15 miles, and a lot of it will be hill climbs. And you're going to love this: Our first destination is Lake of the Isles."

"Lake of the Isles? Just like back in Minneapolis?" she laughed.

"I think in name only." He laughed, too.

"Then where after that?"

"Sonja recommended a little fishing village on the coast. It's called Light's End."

As they rode down the street, Lucia kept one eye on the road and the other on the cat highway above her head. Even though it was already midmorning, many of the shops they passed were closed so the Lylians could ready themselves for the next day's Cat Festival. The few stores that were open sold food and were packed with people buying groceries to prepare feasts for the next day.

They came upon a pastry shop with a long line of hungry faces outside and decided to stop to find out why the shop was so popular. The pastries displayed in the window were spectacular. There were small cakes shaped like cats in every pose imaginable. There were pink-iced cats resting like tiny sphinxes. Others showed cats ready to pounce, claws decorated with blue icing and yellow sprinkles. Some showcased cats in little saddles made up of ornately piped frosting.

Lucia's mouth watered, despite her large breakfast. "Dad, we are definitely stopping here on the way back," she said.

They continued on their ride through the city. Lucia's interest in the paving stones had not lessened, and now she noticed them changing to yet another design, a diamond shape. Nikita hadn't told her the name of this district, but she assumed the pattern must have some meaning.

They soon approached the Crescent River near its junction with the Nigel River. They bicycled across the river on the Eight-Man

Bridge. Nikita had explained the odd name the day before when they had sailed under it. Lucia explained to her dad that the name came from the simple fact that it was designed to be eight men wide. It was also very old.

A few blocks past the river, buildings and houses remained but grew fewer and fewer. Soon the hills became very steep and the city gave way to cliffs, forests and pastures. Their biking became more difficult as the narrow road twisted its way around the mountainside following the Nigel on their left. The river originated in Lake of the Isles, and they followed it to its source.

Thankfully the road had very little traffic that day. But now, from behind them, they heard a low whirring sound become louder until suddenly around the bend came a tightly packed group of 15 or 20 cyclists pedaling for all they were worth. Lucia and her dad jumped back in surprise as the pack raced by them.

"*Zurzavar Hoz Ellenség!*" a few shouted, as they flew past and up the road. "*Zurzavar Hoz Ellenség!*"

"I don't think we'll be catching up to them anytime soon," Leo said with a laugh. "And what so you think they were shouting?"

"I don't think I could ride five seconds with them," Lucia said, stopping at the side of the road. "But I know what they were shouting," she said smugly.

"And that would be …?" he asked.

"*Zurzavar Hoz Ellenség! Confusion to the enemy!*" Lucia shouted. She raised her fist, laughing.

"Let me guess. You learned this from Nikita?"

"*Confusion to the enemy!*" Lucia squeezed her water bottle at her father, and with a squeal raced away laughing even harder.

After several hours of challenging biking and a stop for lunch by

Lake of the Isles—which was as beautiful as Sven said it would be—they arrived at Light's End.

Sonja's promised picturesque village did not disappoint. Small and wrapped along the steep edge of the island, it was very quaint and quite old, with buildings no taller than a story or two. The one exception was a massive old relic of a castle or fort, an ancient edifice looming from the top of a tall peak on the west of town. Its round structure dominated the skyline of Light's End, standing over five stories tall. What remained of the roof seemed like a jagged scar, as though it had been bombed.

There were several large, round openings that must have been windows at one time, easily 20 feet in diameter. Looking through, you could see the walls of the tower were at least 10 feet thick and tapered as the castle rose into the air. It was dark and mysterious, and it was certainly the oldest thing on the island.

"Do you think that relic has anything to do with the town's name?" Leo asked.

"Only if the town were called Creepsville," Lucia said.

They parked their bikes by a small square with a fountain. In it, a statue depicted two ships engaged in a sea battle, their cannons glaring at each other as the crew of one ship prepared to board the other, all of this cast in bronze, now green with age.

"First stop, something cold to drink!" Leo said.

They grabbed their valuables from the bikes and left in search of refreshments.

Looking through his store window, Miklos could not believe his eyes.

They were here. Somehow the American and his daughter had been delivered right into his hands. But he had no way to capture them. It was too soon. The landing party wouldn't be here until tomorrow. And without them no part of the plan could begin. *But they were right here!* Just steps outside his tobacco shop.

There must be something he could do, he thought. Perhaps if he could delay them. He would send his nephew to follow them and find out what they were doing in Light's End.

As the two wandered off, Miklos got an inspiration to steal their bikes.

"If I can disrupt their visit," he thought, "they might need to stay overnight here. I just need them here for another 24 hours."

There was a bed and breakfast in town where they could stay. He thought, if nothing else, he would inconvenience them greatly, which brought a smile to his weathered old face.

Miklos peered out the dirty window onto the square, waiting for the few people around to leave. When no one was looking, he rushed out of the tobacco shop, grabbed their bikes and hid them in the back room of his shop.

"This just might work," he said to himself, and took a long draw from his pipe.

Lucia and Leo walked through the village. There were little shops that sold locally made scrimshaw, not carved out of ivory but from coral that came in many different colors and varieties. There were sea sponges of various sizes, shapes and colors as well to buy.

Lucia and Leo soon found themselves at the town's edge on the sea. Some 200 feet below them the water crashed violently against the steep cliffs. They stood, mesmerized by the sea's churning fury. They finally broke away and walked a short distance to an outdoor café, which allowed them to continue watching the ocean while they rested. The skies had now clouded up again, and on the horizon they could see streaks of lightning illuminate the ominous gray sky.

"Dad, Nikita told me that the land here is like Swiss cheese."

"That's true, Lucia. It really wasn't until the last century, after World War I, that scientists invented the technology that helped them figure out what caused the terrible seas. A guy named Paul Langevin invented SONAR, which stands for sound navigation and ranging..."

"*Dad please,* not a history lecture!"

"All right, but facts are important. The thing is, science could tell us what caused the turbulent seas, but has never been able to tell us how to calm them. Mother Nature always stays one step ahead of us."

Lucia looked out at the ocean and considered the wonders of Mother Nature, which led her to think of her own mother, back home.

"What do you think Mom is up to right now?" she asked.

"I imagine she is probably working in the garden," he said. "We can call her when we get back to the hotel."

"I'd like that a lot. I miss her."

It was midafternoon, and Lucia almost dreaded the ride back to Corvinus. The skies were very dark now, and it looked for certain it would rain.

Miklos' nephew returned panting from his run through the street.

"Uncle, they are coming back to the square, and I think they are getting ready to return to Corvinus," the boy said.

"Well, they won't get far without their bikes," Miklos said. True, there were paddlewheels and even a few water taxis, but with the upcoming holiday, they ran sporadically. Miklos smiled with anticipation of their discomfort. With luck they will have to stay at the bed and breakfast a few blocks away, under his watchful eye. Happy with himself for delaying the visitors and making their capture that much easier, Miklos was certain the Count would be impressed—and that he would be generous in his reward. After all, Miklos was one of the Count's most loyal secret agents on the island. He closed his eyes and day-dreamed of the Count's generosity as he puffed on his pipe.

As they approached the square, Leo was busy studying the map, checking if there might be a quicker route home.

"Dad, is this the right place? Where are the bikes?"

The distinctive fountain with the two ships engaged in sea battle was there. She was sure she recognized the tobacconist shop across from it when they had parked their bikes. The shop was so small and decrepit she had wondered how you could make any money there at all. No, this was the place, and everything was just as they left it, except for the missing bicycles. Lucia clutched her backpack, shuddering at the thought of it disappearing along with the bikes.

Leo looked around to make certain they were in the right place and concluded they were.

"Peanut, I'm sorry. I didn't think we would need to lock them up. I even asked Sonja before we left, and she assured me that a lock wouldn't be necessary."

"Let's ask around," Lucia said. "I'll try that store, and you try the one over there." She walked toward the tobacconist on the corner.

She entered the store and heard the little bell on the door jangle, announcing her entrance. It took a moment for her eyes to adjust to the dim light. She looked around the dark, cluttered room and didn't like it. The air was heavy with the odor of old cigars and pipe tobacco. Around the room were stacks of cigar boxes, cigarette packs and loose tobacco. There was a small glass display case holding carved pipes, cigarette cases and lighters. On the floor beside the case was a disgusting-looking spittoon.

At first the store seemed unoccupied, but then she noticed a red glow and saw an old man sitting on a stool in the corner of the shop, smoking a long white clay pipe and glaring at her. He was dressed in a Moroccan robe and wore on his head a dirty red fez with a tassel that hung down his back. His stare felt different. This one wasn't a curious stare; it was a hateful one.

"*Mit akarsz?*" He asked with a snarl.

"I'm sorry, I don't speak Lylianese. Could you help me? My father and I parked our bikes outside less than an hour ago, and now they're gone. Did you see anyone take them?"

"*Elmegy!*" He waved his pipe at her to leave.

"Sheesh, sorry to have bothered you."

"And stay out of my shop!" the man whispered to himself in English as Lucia left.

Lucia joined her dad near the fountain.

"No luck with that place. Should we report this to the police?"

"I think we can do that back at the hotel," said Leo. "The more important thing to do is find a way back. Let's ask around for transportation options."

"Don't bother with the tobacco shop," Lucia advised. "That old guy was the first rude person I've met here."

"Well the couple I talked with at the bookstore hadn't noticed anything one way or the other about our bikes, but at least they were pleasant. Let's go ask them for advice."

At the bookstore they explained their predicament.

"It sounds like someone wanted to *make you a special!*" the bookshop owner said. He laughed at his own joke. He was a rotund man, dressed as though he had stepped out of a Dickens novel. His wife, dressed in a similar style, gave him a jab to the ribs with her elbow, causing him to wince in pain and stifle his laughter.

"I am so sorry your bicycles have ridden off by themselves," the owner's wife said. "But I'm certain they will turn up. This is a rarity here, but we are not immune to crime, even in Light's End."

"What's the best way back to Corvinus?" Leo asked.

"Well, you are in luck," the shop owner said, rubbing his side. "I have a parcel of books to bring into Corvinus to a client and I would be happy to have you join me on the trip. We'll go by water taxi."

"Oh, that would be great. Thank you so much," Lucia said.

"My name's Porthos, and this is my beautiful bride, Anne," the man said.

"Thank you so much. I'm Leo Boyd and this is my daughter, Lucia."

"Give me just a moment, and we'll be off. Snoop around if you like."

Lucia took him at his word and spent the time looking around the bookstore. She found a small picture book of Lylian, which she purchased as a souvenir. Anne gave her three postcards as a gift, and Lucia thanked her profusely.

"Well, if you are ready, let's be off," Porthos said. He pecked his wife goodbye on the cheek. Lucia and Leo followed him out of the store.

Anne watched the three disappear around a corner. Satisfied they were gone, she poured herself a cup of tea, set a chair near the front window, and sat down with pen, paper and binoculars, ready to record any activity at the tobacconist store.

It didn't take long for her to spy Miklos watching helplessly through the window as the foreigners with the bookseller, arms full of books, made their way down the street to the water taxi stand, got in and floated away.

"Blast it, their goes my reward!" he snarled.

CHAPTER TWENTY-ONE

April 23, 5:38 P.M., On the River Bela Lylian

As THEY FLOATED DOWN THE NARROW RIVER, Porthos spoke merrily about the flora and fauna of the countryside around them, and Lucia could not help feeling a little pleased they didn't have to pedal their bikes back. The trip was not very long, but the hills had been mammoth. She felt like she had trained for the *Tour de France*.

"Are you enjoying our little country?" Porthos asked Lucia.

"More than you can imagine," she replied. "It's so different from just about anywhere. And I saw a Lytle!"

"You are most fortunate indeed. They are quite amazing. Do you know there are some Lylians on the island who would like to see them all destroyed?" he asked?

"*What? No way!* Why in the world would anyone—*I mean anyone*—want to hurt them?"

"Even the Lytles have enemies," he said. "But those who wish them harm know the Lytles are far more dangerous than they appear."

Lucia thought back to her brief encounter with them and how calm they seemed and how comfortable they looked astride their cats. That one Mek, Aranck, *did* seem pretty good with his sword. But really, she used to have dolls taller than him.

"But, Porthos, why would anyone want to get rid of them?"

"Lylian is really not so different from anywhere else in the world that I have read about," he said with a chuckle. "Believe me, I have read a great deal."

Porthos didn't say anything for a few moments, as if gathering his thoughts. They had just cruised through a narrow mountain gorge, and he asked the driver to pull over to the riverbank and stop. It was still light out, but the sun was low in the sky behind them. The clouds had let up substantially, and in the distance they could see more mountains. The wind was cold and refreshing at the same time.

Porthos pointed to the tall mountains out in the distance to the east of them. "Do you see that mountain range?" he asked. "That is *The Tilt.*"

The Boyds took in the distant mountains, dark in shadows and covered in a blanket of deep green forests. There were many peaks, all at different heights, the tallest obscured by clouds. The wind suddenly chilled Lucia to the bone, and she snuggled into her father's side.

"When the island was first sighted by Christopher Corvinus and his party, they knew nothing about the Lytles. They only knew to expect something they'd never seen before and leave their weapons behind. Many in the entourage kept an open mind and were delighted to discover the Lytles. Others were not so generous.

"They were expecting fortunes and felt that they had been tricked into a foolish voyage. Not all of the travelers were looking to start new lives in a new country. That is why I say people are alike everywhere. There are good Lylians, not so good Lylians and those who do not deserve to be called Lylian at all. Some of the families of the fortune hunters kept a deep grudge against the Lytles. Even now. They believe that, thanks to the Lytles, they were brought here for nothing. Over the centuries they have also come to believe The Tilt hides an enormous cache of gold, jewels and even old technology from Atlantis. There are not many of them, but from time to time they try their hand at taking control of the island. It is most unfortunate."

"Why didn't they simply leave on the next ship out and return to Europe?" Leo asked.

"Simple. The Lytles wouldn't let them. For 50 years no one left the island. The Lytles took control of the ship and would allow no one to leave. They knew full well that if knowledge of their existence got out to the rest of the world, they would never be safe. My ancestors may have made it safe and alive to Lylian, but they were also prisoners."

"How in the world could they hold off men seven times their size?" Lucia asked.

"That's what some of the fortune hunters thought as well. At one point they hatched a plan to overpower the little people. The Lytles found out and, using hand gestures, signaled they wanted to put on an exhibition for the humans. The men laughed among themselves but settled down in a clearing of trees by the shore to watch the little combatants.

"What they watched was a display of such skill in swordsmanship, cat riding and cavalry maneuvers that they soon realized they would lose this fight. And then, when they looked around to the forest edge, they discovered thousands of armed Lytles and their cats watching them. So they were outnumbered as well. They now knew they were no match for this fierce race. And so, without a drop of blood, the Lytles conquered the humans."

"That exhibition is credited as the first Cat Festival," Porthos said. "It is a time to celebrate our common bond of friendship but also a time for the Lytles to remind us that this is their island, and after almost 500 years, we are still their guests."

The night was dark now as the sun disappeared on the horizon. Lucia thought of the amazing strength of the Lytles. "What happened next?" she asked.

"After 50 years or so, both groups began to trust and understand each other. They developed a common language and culture. They started to believe in each other. The Lytles eventually realized the humans needed contact with the outside world, and that while away, the humans would keep their secret."

"What about the troublemakers now? What happens to them? Do you put them in jail?"

"No, my dear girl, we do something much worse." Porthos said. "We banish them."

"Like Napoleon to Elba?" Leo asked.

"Napoleon was exiled *to* an island for punishment. Here troublemakers are removed *from* the island," Porthos said. "For a Lylian, any Lylian, to be banished forever from our island and all that we hold dear? That is a very big price to pay."

"Where do you send them?" Lucia asked. "What stops them from talking?"

"Various countries, depending on the culprit. Sometimes Hungary. Sometimes South Africa. We have means to put them just about anywhere we like. If they ever were to tell our secrets, they would no longer be banished. They would be dead."

Lucia gulped a bit. "This group, do they have a name?"

"They refer to themselves as *A Törvényes*, The Rightful. We true Lylians refer to them as fools."

CHAPTER TWENTY-TWO

April 23, 6:35 P.M., Corvinus, Lylian

THE TRIP BACK WAS CONSIDERABLY SHORTER than the bike ride that preceded it. The water taxi with the fat Lylian bookseller pulled up to a docking station, just a few blocks from their hotel, and the two Americans got out.

"Porthos, I cannot thank you enough," Leo said.

"Nonsense, it was my pleasure," Porthos responded. "Besides, as I said, I had business in the city."

"And thanks for the Lytle information," Lucia said. "I just can't get enough of it."

"Enjoy your stay," he said, and the water taxi cruised away.

"Come on, Lucia, we have some explaining to do," Leo said.

Entering the hotel, the Boyds approached Sven, standing at the reception desk. Before they could mention the stolen bikes, Sven put down his paper and said, "Ah, Mr. Boyd, Miss Lucia, I'm glad to see you made it back safely. Terribly sorry to hear about the stolen bikes. Most unfortunate. But I assure you, they will turn up."

"How did you know?" Lucia asked. "We didn't even tell the police. We just bummed a ride home."

"Yes, well, it is a small island, Miss Lucia. As it happens, we received a telephone call from a bookstore in Light's End that informed us of the theft and that you were being escorted home by the proprietor."

Lucia loved a good mystery, and this was right up her alley. Even as a young girl, while others put on make-believe tea parties, Lucia was solving make-believe crimes and rescuing dolls from imminent peril.

"Sven, who would *steal* our bikes?" she said.

"I'm certain just kids having fun. They will turn up. Now, if you will excuse me, I need to attend to a few things."

"Thanks for the help, Sven," Leo said. "By the way, Lake of the Isles was absolutely beautiful."

"It was my pleasure, and I will inform Sonja of your predicament in Light's End. I am certain she will want to know. By the way, you received some mail today. I took the liberty of bringing it up to your room. Good evening."

"Dad, I'm tired, dirty and hungry," Lucia said as they climbed the stairs to their room.

"That's all easy to fix," Leo replied. "Let's shower up, relax for a bit, and then I suggest we walk back to the square where we had dinner the first night and try another restaurant."

Lucia went over to look at their mail. It was a single large envelope that was clearly an invitation to something. The paper was thick and a creamy blue with tiny gold flecks. It was addressed in flowing cursive handwriting to *Mr. Leonardo Boyd & Miss Lucia Boyd*. The flap was sealed in back with a large dollop of deep blue wax into which the seal of Lylian had been pressed. Lucia carefully opened it to avoid harming the seal. Inside she found a very formal invitation printed on the same paper. On the cover of the invitation was the seal of Lylian printed in green foil, just like the visa in her passport.

She opened the card to read:

His Excellency, The Navigator
Jakob Diego Guido Corvinus (Retired)
Cordially Invites You To
Celebrate The Cat Festival
With The Corvinus Family.
Festivities Will Begin At The Family Home At One P.M.
With Lunch, Entertainment and Relaxation.
At Six P.M., Transportation Will Be Provided To
Dinner In Town, Prior To The Parade.

In the corner of the invitation appeared a handwritten note: "Lucia, sorry for the last-minute invitation. I hope you and your dad can make it. Give me a call and I'll send a car. Best, Nikita." Beside her signature was a phone number.

"Ohmygosh. Ohmygosh. Dad! *Dad!*" she yelled.

Leo burst out of his room, his face covered in shaving cream.

"What?" He said looking around expecting to see an intruder.

"This. This is what." She pushed the invitation into his face to read. "I told you Nikita was no ordinary girl. Her dad was a Navigator. That's like he was the secretary of state! That's second only to the President, I mean the Captain! And Dad, her last name, she's a Corvinus! She's like royalty or something."

"Lucia, settle down. I know. I knew who he was when we were meeting yesterday. I didn't tell you because I wanted you to act like your normal, goofy self around Nikita instead of acting even goofier and treating her like nobility. She puts her boots on one leg at a time, just like you."

"Yes, but have you seen her boots? They're beautiful. Oh, Dad. I just have to call her now and tell her I wouldn't miss it for the world,"

Lucia said, reaching for the phone.

"*Corvinus rezidencia,*" said the voice on the other end of the phone.

"Yes, hello, may I please speak to Nikita Corvinus?" Lucia said.

"*Egy pillanat.* One moment please."

In a few minutes Lucia heard another phone receiver being picked up.

"Hi Lucia," Nikita said. "You got the invitation?"

"We did. I did. Thank you so much. It sounds like so much fun. We would love to come. Can we bring anything? Is it formal? I mean what should we wear? I didn't bring any really fancy clothes along."

"There is nothing you need to bring, and the dress code is very relaxed. It is a perfect time to wear your new boots."

"I have them on right now. Dad and I are going out for dinner, and I just love them. Wait until I tell you about today. We went on a bike trip and our bikes were stolen in Light's End."

"Stolen? On Lylian? *Someone made you a special.*"

Leo and Lucia walked the now familiar streets to the square. At the far end they selected a small restaurant that specialized in seafood. It wasn't Lucia's favorite thing to eat, but she managed to find something on the menu.

As they ate dinner she kept her eye on the cat roads over her head but saw only an occasional cat go by. She figured they were all at home getting ready for the big day tomorrow.

During the meal Lucia remembered the pastry shop they passed earlier in the day. It was just a few blocks away, and she insisted to her dad that they stop after dinner to pick up some pastries to bring to the party.

They were lucky enough to find it still open and still selling the small cat cakes. Lucia purchased a dozen in various poses, and they headed back to The Matthias.

After Porthos left the docking station he had the water taxi take him and the same stack of books he had pretended needed delivery directly back to Light's End along the dark and winding river.

"That was very close, very close," he said to his wife as he entered their shop. He then positioned himself in the darkened bookstore to keep an eye on the tobacconist shop across the square.

"Just blind luck that it occurred right by us," Anna said.

Porthos had recognized Lucia the moment she walked into his store. As a member of the island's governing council, Porthos was well aware of who Lucia was and the importance of her visit to Lylian. Porthos speculated on the consequences to the Americans had they fallen into the hands of *The Rightful*. The thought made him shudder.

CHAPTER TWENTY-THREE

April 24, 5:31 A.M., Lake Neusiedler, Austria

COUNT JOSEPH EUGENE SAVOY was up very early and beside himself with anticipation. In just hours, Vladimir would be landing the Count's army on the island.

"Just hours away," he said to himself, arranging the pencils on his desk for the hundredth time.

The Count sat in his Control Center, adjacent to the coyote training kennel. There had been limited contact with Vladimir and the submarine since their departure earlier in the month. Occasionally Vladimir came up to periscope depth to send quick coded messages that they were safe and still in position. The Count now waited for one final signal from the submarine indicating the start of the invasion.

Working behind the scenes irritated him. He had thought about joining the invasion crew and leading them into battle, but he knew his limitations. Besides, if things did not work out as he had hoped and he was captured, it would mean certain death. The Banished are to never return.

"Ah, but the Banished *will* return," he said to the walls. "When we do, we will join our brothers, *The Rightful*, and take what is ours, rightfully ours—*everything.*"

While the Count waited for the final coded message from the

submarine he thought inwardly what a stroke of good fortune it had been to find Vladimir.

"It's a pity he won't be returning," the Count thought to himself.

Suddenly the Count's computer screen lit up with a message. He read the screen, his eyes wide with interest.

"It has begun," he whispered. The submarine was making its approach.

Chapter Twenty-Four

April 24, 10:31 A.M., Off the North Coast of Lylian

"Bring us to periscope depth," Vladimir commanded the submarine helmsman.

Vladimir wanted one last look at the pre-dawn sky before he went into the seas of hell itself.

Peering through the periscope, he spun to look behind him to the calm waters of the open Atlantic Ocean. How peaceful it looks, he thought. Then he rotated to look in the direction he would be sailing. In the distance he could see the shore of Lylian pummeled by enormous waves. Between him and the shore he saw nothing but chaos. Swirling waves battled each other. Charcoal skies loomed overhead.

"Let us see how well Mother Russia trains her Navy," he said to himself. He flipped a switch, and a quick pulse of encrypted information went beaming off to the Count.

Vladimir lowered the periscope back into the submarine. "We are going to do what we came for. May God have mercy on us. Prepare to dive. *Battle stations.*"

The combat lights of the K487 bathed the crew in an eerie red glow. Occasionally the sub would lurch and emergency sirens would begin to blare. Vladimir went to his safe and removed the documents that were supposed to lead him safely through the waters.

"I have read these orders over and over, and they appear sheer madness," he said to the helmsman. "We will follow exactly what they say, but if at any time these orders challenge the safety of this vessel, we abort the mission. Is that understood?"

"Aye, Captain," the helmsman said.

Vladimir left the bridge to personally warn the mercenaries they were preparing to land. In the background he could hear those infernal coyotes the Count insisted were vital to the mission. Even secured behind steel hatches several cabins away, he could still hear them howling 24 hours a day. True, they were not used to life at sea and being cooped up for so long, but their unceasing noise was putting everyone's nerves on edge. Vladimir thought it would be worth it alone to land on Lylian just to get rid of the coyotes.

Vladimir found the mercenary leader, Horatio Simon "Red" White, in his cabin. Red earned his nickname from his thick red hair, kept cut military style.

"It is time," Vladimir said. "I have given the orders to go in. With any luck, you, your men—and those blasted coyotes—will be ashore in a matter of an hour or two. That, or we will all be guests of Davy Jones. Are your men ready?"

"We've been ready for months. Just get this bucket of bolts close to shore and let us take it from there," Red snarled.

Red finished cleaning his gun and then reassembled it in a matter of seconds, his eyes never leaving Vladimir's face. The Count had found Red, an ex-U.S. Army gunnery sergeant, locked in a Moroccan prison accused of dealing in illegal weapons. The Count had arranged for his release with the stipulation that he work for him—doing whatever the Count asked. Vladimir left the mercenary and returned to the bridge.

"I'm getting too old for this," Vladimir said to himself.

Satisfied his weapon was in perfect working order, Red went to gather his troops and go over last-minute preparations.

"Men, you know why we're here," he said to the assembled group.

"Yeah, 'cause we're being paid a ton of money," one of the mercenaries shouted, and they all laughed.

"Well, now it's time to earn it," Red said with a snarl. "This ain't gonna be no cake walk. When I say you might not make it to land, it ain't no empty threat."

The submarine lurched and pitched as it began its entry into the explosive waters of Lylian. Plates flew off the tables, and several men staggered and fell. The coyotes were suddenly very quiet.

"Look sharp," he yelled over the sound of the emergency sirens blaring above their heads. "Pack up your gear! Get the coyotes ready. I want them muzzled, and I want them in their leather socks. One scratch or bite from them on your inflatable Zodiac and it becomes your coffin. Move smartly. Now."

The men gave a shout of "Yes, Sir" and began their final preparations as the boat spun them left and right.

Vladimir studied his charts and his instruments. He cared little if the men made it to shore or not. His job was to get them close and out of the sub. After that it was up to them; his only goal was to make it back out to open sea alive. "It's every man for himself," he thought.

The submarine lurched again as the heavy currents buffeted the boat around like a toy.

"Captain, I've never seen seas like this before. I think we may have to abort," the helmsman said, holding onto a control panel for dear life.

"Stay your course. We're not giving up yet," Vladimir ordered.

The submarine continued to bobble around in the churning seas. Crewmen would turn off the wailing emergency sirens only for another calamity to trip them again. From the mercenaries could be heard the frightened cries of grown men. The stench of vomit filled the air.

The steel skin of the submarine began to groan as the ship twisted round and around. Pipes broke overhead and steam and water filled the cabin. Vladimir barked out orders to seal any open pipes and maintained his heading according to the plans. Several crewmen, tossed by the violent motion of the boat, had open gashes on their foreheads and were being tended by fellow mates as best they could.

"Captain!" the helmsman screamed. "We must turn around. You'll kill us all!"

Vladimir paid him no mind. He was busy counting. The last big lurch, the one that almost crushed them, had been the 11th major hit to the sub. Now he was counting time on his stopwatch and checking their depth.

"Helmsman, on my mark take us to heading 33 degrees and emergency surface!" Vladimir yelled at the top of his voice.

Vladimir looked at his watch, studied the chart and counted, "Three, two, one …" he shouted. "Helmsman … NOW!"

The submarine began its ascent.

CHAPTER TWENTY-FIVE

April 24, 11:22 A.M., Corvinus, Lylian

"COME OUTSIDE WITH ME," Leo said. "I want to show you something."

Lucia reluctantly put away her pen and closed her book. "What?" she said. Lucia had slept-in that morning and was updating her journal on all that had happened.

Leo led her downstairs, through the lobby and out to the street. Lucia looked around in disbelief.

The city had been transformed.

From every building hung huge banners of blue with the national crest. Lylian flags flew from every street corner. Giant blue bunting lined the main streets in large looping waves. At every doorstep sat a large, welcoming saucer of milk. It was a party waiting to happen.

Some islanders had already engaged the party spirit. Groups of people danced through the streets, playing guitars and other instruments, laughing and singing, fueled by an early-morning glass of *Kék Bor*. All were dressed in their finest and gaudiest clothes. And all of them wore at least one blue item. It might be a pair of bright blue boots, or an elaborately embroidered blue vest. One loudly singing couple was completely outfitted in blue clothing.

As the Boyds wandered the tiny side streets around their hotel, they looked through the windows and saw that, in many of the houses, furniture had been moved aside to fill the room with long and elegantly decorated banquet tables. Some sat 20 or more. These rooms were decorated with blue lanterns and crepe paper.

This looks like so much fun, Lucia thought, and then remembered she had her own special party to go to.

"Dad, let's go. The car will be here soon, and we have to get ready," she implored, tugging on his sleeve and dragging him back toward the hotel.

Once they entered their room, Leo tossed a small shopping bag to Lucia.

"Here, I thought you might want this."

Lucia opened the bag and tore through the blue tissue paper. Folded inside lay a white pirate's shirt with a tiny pattern of blue cats and a deep blue embroidered vest with a matching pattern in lighter blue.

"*Ohmygosh*, Dad, this is perfect!" She screamed, hugging him in thanks.

"Peanut, we can't out-class them, but at least we can out-dress them," he said. He then made a low mock bow. Leo was wearing his best dark blue suit, white shirt and a new blue tie he had purchased for himself while Lucia was out with Nikita.

"Dad, you look just fine. But come on. I don't want to keep the car waiting."

Lucia grabbed the box of cat pastries and pushed her dad out of the hotel, backpack in hand. They waited only minutes in the lobby until a very, very old car pulled up to the curb. It was long, navy blue and looked ancient.

"Lucia, this is what movie stars in the 1930s used to drive around in," Leo said.

The driver got out of the car and opened the door for them. "In you go, then. We'll be there in a jiff," he said with a thick Lylian accent.

Lucia and Leo got into the back of the car and sank into old blue leather that reeked with age. Their compartment was completely contained from the driver. The glass barrier separating them was rolled down, and they watched the driver get into the car.

"Settled in, are we?" he asked. "Hang on, off we go."

The car motored away from the hotel and soon joined what, for the island at least, was busy traffic.

"Everybody is out today, going this way and that," the driver said. He looked at them through the rearview mirror, oblivious of traffic. "Isn't it your favorite time of year?"

"It is now," Lucia said. "This is our first Cat Festival!"

"Your first? Aren't you in for a bit of a treat! At the Navigator's no less! You must be doing something right."

He drove the car over the Matthias Bridge onto Béla Island and then over to Matthias Island. Lucia saw that the island was small and very hilly. Scattered among the hills were many government buildings, forming a near fortress. Some looked like ancient Grecian temples, while others would be more at home just off of Pall Mall in old London. Among the buildings stood stately residential structures. The architecture here varied less than in Lylian proper, but it was just as appealing.

The buildings were very old and, for the most part, built of stone. Many seemed to grow right out of the hillside. They peppered the rolling hillsides and were constructed on any piece of land that would accommodate them. The houses lined up neatly along the winding streets, but as the hills rose, they became more scattered. Many were perched on the sides of craggy cliffs and were connected to the road by long, winding driveways.

"Almost there," the driver said cheerily.

He made a left off the main road and drove up a steep, curvy lane populated with lavishly gated houses almost obscured by tall stone walls.

The driver continued the ascent until he came to an iron gate held in place by massive pillars with an iron crow topping each. He pressed a remote control, and the heavy iron gate slowly opened and allowed them entrance. The car continued to climb up a last steep road. As it turned a corner, the Corvinus family house came into view—if something that magnificent can be called a house. Mansion would be more like it, or starter castle, Lucia thought. It wasn't that it was that large, even though the Boyd family home would fit nicely into any one of its rooms. It's just that it was so elegant. It looked like it had been shipped over from Europe stone by stone. It was constructed of pale stone, three stories high, with many windows, gables and balconies. The main entrance graced the center of the building, surrounded by tall multi-paned windows. On the right side of the house was a large leaded-glass solarium. The driver brought the car around the horseshoe driveway and stopped at the front entrance. To the left were several parked cars and four sleek black motorcycles.

As Lucia and Leo got out of the car, the massive carved oak door of the house opened, and out stepped Nikita.

"Lucia. Don't you look great," Nikita said. She hugged her friend.

A moment later Nikita's father came out as well. "Leo, Lucia— welcome, welcome," he said. "The timing of your visit couldn't be better. It's going to be a great Cat Festival."

"Mr. Navigator, thank you so much for inviting my daughter and me," Leo said. He attempted some sort of bow.

"Leo, please call me Jakob. Lucia, I can see the island style agrees with you. Come follow me."

Lucia and Leo followed Nikita and the Navigator into the beautiful house. The reception hall was very large and as equally impressive as the exterior, with marble floors and tapestry-covered walls. To their left rose a curving staircase, and in front of them a bank of French doors extended the width of the room.

"Oh, I almost forgot, these are for you," Lucia said and handed the pastries to Nikita. "It's not much."

"Aren't you nice. Thank you," Nikita looked inside the box and smiled. "These are my favorite. Now let's go out to the garden. That's where the party is!"

Nikita linked Lucia's arm and walked her out through the French doors, while Leo and the Navigator, talking amicably, followed behind.

The house was U-shaped, with a wing on each side of the reception hall and a large courtyard in the center. The expansive courtyard was paved but included sections for lawn, trees and flowerbeds. In the center of the courtyard, a large, long table had been profusely set to serve 20 people for lunch. The table was decorated in shades of blue, including translucent blue vases holding bouquets of blue and yellow flowers. Most of the guests had already arrived and were milling about in groups, talking and laughing.

At the end of the courtyard, granite steps led down to a rolling, manicured, tree-lined lawn that stopped at the shores of a lake and grand dock. Tied to the dock were several boats of various sizes and designs.

"Nikita, this is so awesome," Lucia said. I knew you weren't just any ordinary girl,"

"Oh, please, Lucia. I hate that. I am just an ordinary girl. Come, I want to introduce you to everybody."

They joined Leo, who was now surrounded by a small group of people as Jakob made introductions.

"Leo and Lucia Boyd, I'd like you to meet my oldest friend and trusted advisor, Wan Foo Chan, and his wife, MeLee. The Boyds are from America, and this is their first time to Lylian."

All shook hands, and Lucia noticed the Chans were dressed in fairly traditional Chinese garb, except they both wore red high-tops.

Another man and his wife joined the party, walking through the French doors and up to the Navigator. "Sorry to be late, Jakob, the city is already a madhouse, and the streets are jammed with people celebrating. Traffic is terrible."

"But you're here now, Karl," Jakob said. That's what counts. Swan, you look beautiful. " He introduced the Boyds and immediately Karl began asking Leo dozens of questions about America.

Nikita and Lucia slipped away and headed toward the lake to say hello to Laszlo, who was talking with friends.

"Nikita, it is so beautiful here. Your house and these gardens are so cool. I hate using that word, but I can't think of anything else. Is it very old?"

"This house is about 300 years old. There was a smaller one here before that, but it burned down in the fires. Much of the island was destroyed in fires back then. But that is a story for another day."

They crossed the lawn and joined Laszlo, who for the first time that Lucia could remember, was smartphone-free.

"Hey, Lucia, glad you could make it," Laszlo said. Lucia blushed instantly. "This is the American I was telling you about." Laszlo introduced her to his four friends, Katie, Charles, Hannah and Emmett. They all appeared to be in their 20s, right around Laszlo's age. They said hello and made her feel welcome. Lucia noticed that while everyone else at the party had dressed in brilliant blue outfits, Laszlo and his friends wore black, although they accessorized with a bit of blue: a scarf around the neck of Hannah, and a to-die-for blue vest for Katie. Each of them wore a blue armband on their right sleeve.

They were still talking by the dock and skipping rocks into the lake when two late-arriving guests, a boy and a girl about the same age as Nikita, came running across the lawn.

"Nikita! Nikita!" they shouted and ran up to greet her. Clearly they were best friends, and the three began talking a mile a minute in Lylianese.

"Megáll. Megáll! Halt. Halt. English please." Nikita said. "We have a guest from America. Viktoria, Stephan—my new friend, Lucia Boyd."

The two late arrivals looked coolly at Lucia with the classic Lylian stare. Then both said hello in halting English. It seemed clear to Lucia the two did not like sharing Nikita's friendship.

CHAPTER TWENTY-SIX

April 24, 1:00 P.M., Off the North Coast of Lylian

THE SHIP'S WARNING SIREN SHRILLED again as the crew braced for surfacing through the heavy seas that continued to threaten the submarine as it rolled and bounced. But then, suddenly, the waters calmed. The hull stopped groaning and the pummeling stopped. Less than a hundred feet from the ocean's surface, the waters completely normalized.

The submarine surfaced 300 yards off the coast of Lylian, a few miles from Light's End. Vladimir had landed the mercenaries within 100 feet of his target destination. Those of the crew that weren't still vomiting or weren't unconscious from hitting their heads let out a cheer that could raise the dead.

Vladimir had done it. He had breached the waters of Lylian, the second outsider to do so in almost 500 years.

"*Spasiba*. Thank you, Russian Naval Academy," he said to no one. Then just as quickly he shouted at the mercenaries, "Hurry! *For the love of God, hurry!* You have minutes to get off the boat before the sea engulfs us again."

While the assault team prepared to disembark, several of Vladimir's crew went up through the conning tower and released the Zodiac inflatable vessels from the dry-dock storage container atop the boat. They hit the inflate button. In a matter of moments, the 10

Zodiacs were fully operational. Each was equipped with a small but powerful electric motor, very fast but good for less than a mile. That was more than enough to reach the shore.

Each man carried two packs, one holding weapons, spare ammunition, rappelling rope and harness, medical supplies, maps, compass, water, energy bars and coyote food, the other containing a canvas sling holding a coyote. The coyotes were trussed into the slings so they couldn't move and cause the soldier to lose balance. Sedating them for the voyage was not an option, since the coyotes would not have recovered in time for the mission.

"Men. Line up by team. Now! Up and out! Go," Red commanded. The 40 men, a coyote trussed in front of each, prepared to leave the sub. Several of them were still seasick from the rough ride, and more than one had to be held up by others.

"Come on," Red said. "It's time to earn this lovely ocean cruise. Move it!" They passed quickly out of the boat, each group of four jumping into a Zodiac, casting off and immediately racing at high speed for shore. The sun was just breaking the horizon, and with any luck they would all be on shore before they could be spotted.

"Prepare for emergency dive!" Vladimir shouted. He headed back down into the boat, securing the hatch. He got this far, he thought, and said a prayer that he could get back out.

"My God, the weather here changes fast," Red thought as he headed toward shore. Already the relatively calm water began to churn. In a matter of moments the waves were cresting at 15 feet. He was less than 50 yards from shore now, but the swells were so great he could see it only between periods of complete blindness.

He looked around to see how the other boats were doing. Two Zodiacs had already landed, and the eight men were dragging them ashore to hide them in a thicket of bushes. About 70 feet to the right was a lone Zodiac, and farther from him, spaced about 50 feet apart, were three more. He looked behind him and saw the remaining three, one clearly having engine trouble.

"I'll be much happier when we're all on shore," he shouted to the man next to him over the din of the motor and now-raging waters.

Suddenly, the inflatable just ahead of Red was picked up by a rogue wave and tossed high overhead. It landed back in the water, upside down.

Red signaled to the boat on his right to save the crew. Meanwhile he looked to the three Zodiacs behind him and waved his arm, signaling them to pick up the speed. The distressed Zodiac's engine had stopped entirely, and he was just coming about to tow it in when, out of nowhere, the water around it grew turbulent and started swirling into a giant whirlpool. The men onboard started paddling with their hands to make an escape.

But it was too late. The sea engulfed the small inflatable and sucked it into the whirlpool's vortex. In a moment the boat and crew were gone.

Red spun around to check the fate of the others. The rescue Zodiac had managed to save two from the water. The two remaining inflatables behind him were in trouble.

Red and the three remaining Zodiacs were in the water only yards from the shore. The eight men already on shore had tethered the coyotes and rushed out into the powerful swells to help as best they could.

Of the last two inflatables, one had neared shore, and the men on shore could see the complete terror still on the faces of its four passengers. The men ran out to grab it and drag it to safety.

The 30 survivors of the 40 original soldier-sailors scanned the horizon in search of the last Zodiac. But it was gone. The landing was over.

The last Zodiac and its crew would not be attending the Cat Festival.

Chapter Twenty-Seven
April 24, 1:30 P.M., Mathias Island, Lylian

SOON LUNCH WAS CALLED and Lucia found her seating card in the middle of the long table with Wan Foo Chan on her left and Katie on her right. Across from her was Nikita with Viktoria and Stephan on either side. The table was full, with the exception of the unoccupied seat next to Jakob. Once everyone was seated, the Navigator stood to welcome his guests and addressed them in Lylianese and then English.

"Dear friends, once again it is time for the Cat Festival," he declared, and the group cheered. "Many of us here have celebrated this day together for over 50 years!" Jakob raised his glass and toasted Wan Foo and MeLee. "Others are here for the first time." He made the same gesture toward the Boyds.

"One day we will all be gone, and others will celebrate in our place. But when they do, they will celebrate the same things we do now: Friendship, the power of The Tilt and the magic of Lylian!"

"Friends join me, *"Zurzavar Hoz Ellenség! Confusion to the enemy!"*

"Zurzavar Hoz Ellenség! Confusion to the enemy!" everyone shouted, jumping to their feet.

With that cry, the French doors flew open and servants came out carrying wine glasses, bottles of *Kék Bor* and platters of food. Soon everyone had a full glass, with orange sodas for those younger.

Huge platters of appetizers were passed family-style, and Wan Foo and Katie insisted that Lucia fill her plate with olives, cheese, and a variety of tiny dumplings filled with meats or vegetables. On the edge of the courtyard a man and woman softly played guitar and violin. Overhead, the sky cycled through dark clouds, warm sun and then back to overcast. A slight breeze blew across the table.

"So tell me, Miss Lucia, are you enjoying our little country?" Wan Foo Chan asked.

"You have no idea!" she said. "Do you know I saw a Lytle? His name is Aranck." She then went on to explain her encounter a few days ago.

"You will get to see more than one tonight," Wan Foo said. He dipped a bit of bread into his *Kék Bor*. "The parade is most enjoyable."

"Will we go to the parade?" she asked.

"No, the parade will come to us," Wan Foo said and laughed.

Before Lucia could ask what he meant, Katie asked Lucia to pass the butter.

"Oh, how I want to visit America," Katie said.

"I would love to have you stay with us," Lucia said. "Why don't you visit?"

"America won't issue travel visas for Lylians," Katie replied. "Because we are so restrictive on whom we allow into our country, your government won't let us into yours. And I so want to see Hollywood."

The servers circled with more wine and soda, but rather than fill the now-empty glasses, they set down new ones to fill. The appetizer platters were removed and replaced with large bowls of sliced fruit and many small bowls of different dipping sauces. Lucia liked the chocolate sour cream the best.

Katie turned to speak to Charles on her right, giving Lucia a chance to look around the table. Everyone was busy talking away and waving their hands. Every once in a while someone would shout out, *"Zurzavar Hoz Ellenség!"* and everyone would say it again in response.

As the lunch continued, the table started filling up with more and more glasses. Lucia wondered how the servers, who seemed to be so attentive to everything else, could not notice the stemware piling up.

"I see you are wondering about the glasses!" Wan Foo said.

"If they keep this up, they're going to run out," Lucia said.

"Run out of glasses? Not at this house, I can assure you. I've been to dinner parties here and seen them stacked to the ceiling. It is a beautiful sight."

"Stacked?"

"It is a tradition. It means you have great wealth—that you can use a glass once and then get a fresh one—you keep them on the table so there is no cheating, no washing ones that have been used."

"How did it start?" Lucia asked.

"Who knows?" Wan Foo laughed. He stabbed his chopstick at a large piece of banana and dipped it into a kiwi sauce. "Tell me, do you know how a color can be lucky?"

"I know that one," Lucia said triumphantly. "When it's a blue lantern and it saves your life!"

"Very good, you are learning our secrets. Now tell me, Miss Lucia, by any chance do you have your passport with you?"

Lucia looked at him, puzzled, and produced her passport from her backpack.

"Ah, American passport, very nice. Did you look at your Lylian visa closely, Miss Lucia?"

"Only every day for a week when I got it," she said.

"Then you are familiar with the Lylian seal right here." He pointed to the heavy sheet of paper printed with metallic green ink, glued into her passport.

"It's also on your flag. It's even on the window of our hotel. It's a crow sitting on the back of a cat."

"Yes, but do you know what it signifies?" Wan Foo asked.

"Well, I suppose the cat signifies all the cats here and the crow must mean, I don't know, cat dinner?"

Wan Foo roared with laughter and slapped his knee. "The bird certainly could be dinner, anytime this cat wants. The cat represents Lylian Island. Did you know that a cat has been the national symbol of this island for thousands of years? Long before Christopher Corvinus landed here, it was the symbol of a much bigger country than you see here now."

"*Atlantis!*" Lucia said.

"Yes, you know so much, you should be teaching me," Wan Foo smiled. "There are still ruins around the island from those who lived here before us. Ancient carvings are all around us, and many are of cats, just like you see here." He pointed to the cat on the visa. "Christopher adopted the ancient symbol to represent the new nation, but added the raven to show that it was a new beginning."

"Why a raven?"

"Christopher was honoring his grandfather, Matthias. *Corvinus* is the Latin word for raven, or crow, as you Americans call them. Corvinus was the nickname given to Matthias by his Black Army. It stuck as the family's last name, and the raven became the family coat of arms."

Lucia studied the passport lying between her and Wan Foo.

"Mr. Chan, look at this tiny piece of paper in the corner," she said. "It's so hard to read. I looked at it back home with a magnifying glass and I couldn't make out any of the letters at all. And the crest has the same cat but no raven on its back."

"You are very observant, Miss Lucia. The large green visa is from Lylian and permits you to enter the country. The small blue one is from the Lytles and says that you have their permission as well. You must have both to visit the island. You see, we are really two countries, living as one."

"The cat is their symbol?"

"Yes. No raven or human will ever sit on the back of any cat or Lytle. Now I believe it is time for the soup course."

The fruit course plates were cleared away, and more drinking glasses were added, gradually building into shimmering, translucent walls. Wan Foo was correct, the next course was soup, with several to choose from. Wan Foo chose a seafood gumbo, and Lucia had corn chowder.

Jakob's brother, sitting at the end of the long table to Lucia's right, raised his glass toward Karl and shouted, "Sing me a song!"

Soon the others joined in shouting, "Sing me a song! *Sing me a song!*"

Karl took a sip of *Kék Bor* and stood up. Everyone quieted down, and then in a clear but deep voice Karl began singing in Lylianese. Lucia didn't understand a word. It started low and slow. As the lyrics progressed he sang louder and with more enthusiasm. Lucia recognized the phrase, *Zurzavar Hoz Ellenség*, but that was all she could make out. As the song neared the end, everyone rose from their chairs and joined in singing the last few bars together. The table cheered and toasted each other. Laszlo, sitting next to Karl, slapped him on the back in thanks.

"That was beautiful," Lucia said to Katie. "What was it about?"

"It is our national song, our anthem," Katie replied. "The words tell about our ancestor pirates landing here safely, but the melody is as old as the island."

The soup bowls were cleared, and then Karl lifted his glass to Jakob's sister-in-law and said, "Sing me a song!" Once again the others joined in shouting, "Sing me a song! *Sing me a song!*"

She rose to her feet, cleared her throat with mock solemnity and began singing in a loud operatic voice the "Toreador Song" from *Carmen*. As she sang, she moved her arms, gesturing with bravada. People started slapping time on the table, and the whole table shook, with glasses clanging—thankfully none breaking. She sat down to tumultuous applause and bowed her head in thanks.

Lucia was starting to figure out the singing game. "Now does she get to ask someone to sing?

"Yes she does, and it could be you, so you better have a song ready." Katie said.

The lunch went on for several hours as clouds continued to roll by. After a slight break, a fish course was presented. Tuna, mussels, scallops and eel. Tureens of bouillabaisse and platters of lobster. Sea bass, crab cakes and small pockets of fried bread prepared with fish in the center. The song game had changed hands several times, the last being Viktoria and Stephan, who sang an old Lylian children's song that had the grown-ups in happy tears. By now the fish course was over and the meat dishes arrived. Lucia wondered if she might explode from all the food.

Lucia was trying to take the smallest portion of beef kabobs, just to be polite, when she saw the French doors open and the final luncheon guest arrive. The man was very tall, thin, yet powerfully built. He was dressed in a somber black suit, shirt and scarf with shiny black leather boots up to his knees. Darkly tanned, he looked like someone who spent a great deal of time outdoors. His hair was thick, white and long, which he wore tied back. In deference to the holiday, a blue armband adorned his right sleeve.

He crossed the courtyard, walking directly to Jakob. As he did so, Laszlo and his four friends stood up at the table in attention. The man acknowledged them with a wave of his hand. They sat back down and started talking quietly to each other.

The man bowed at the waist and addressed the host.

"Navigator, please excuse my very late arrival," he said. "I had official business in Light's End, and it took considerably longer than I had expected."

"Nonsense, General Rutger," Jakob said. "You work far too hard for Lylian. Come sit beside me. You have much food and *Kék Bor* to catch up on!"

Jakob signaled the staff to serve his last guest. While the general waited for his dinner to arrive, the two shared a few quiet words.

After this brief interlude, the party once again returned to conversation, loud laughter and the clinking of glasses. Viktoria and Stephan lifted their juice glasses and pointed them toward Laszlo. "Sing me a song!" Everyone took up the cry and Laszlo stood.

"I will require some backup," he nodded to his four friends who all stood, ready to sing.

"*A Fekete Hadsereg Dal!* The Black Army Song!" Laszlo announced, and the celebrants at the table clapped and cheered. Laszlo began the verse, with his friends joining in on the chorus. Again the table broke out in cheers with calls of "Encore! Encore!"

Food arrived for General Rutger, who wolfed it down like a man starving, while the others were served a salad course. Lucia was pecking away at a leaf of lettuce, trying to find room for it, when Laszlo pointed his glass at Lucia and said, "Sing me a song!"

Instantly everyone was looking to Lucia and shouting the same thing.

She looked to her dad, who urged her up. Lucia stood and

wondered if she could get any words out at all. She had been thinking of a dozen songs she might sing, and now her mind turned blank. She glanced down at Wan Foo, who smiled at her encouragingly. Viktoria and Stephan just smirked, clearly enjoying her discomfort. That look was all the incentive she needed.

Lucia started quietly singing: *In the town where I was born, lived a man who sailed the sea, and he told us of his life, in the land of submarines ...*

As she sang, her confidence grew and her voice became louder and stronger. When she reached the chorus, several sang along with her:

We all live in a yellow submarine, yellow submarine, yellow submarine ...

Lucia continued the song, clearly enjoying herself. This time the entire table, including Nikita's father, joined in on the chorus and continued singing with her until the end. The table cheered even more, and Wan Foo ceremoniously brushed off her chair and held it for her like a throne.

"Well done, Lucia!" they all said.

Even Viktoria and Stephan enjoyed the tune and smiled warmly at her, and Lucia could tell they were going to be friends after all.

"You know the Beatles? she asked Katie.

"But of course. They performed here several times many years ago. My parents saw them. We're not entirely isolated."

Only one person sitting at the table did not enjoy the song as well as the others. General Rutger thought the song on this day a very bad premonition.

Then came the cheese course. This time Lucia made no pretense at all and declined any more to eat. They had been sitting at the table almost four hours.

The cheese course went quickly and was replaced by dessert. The end of the meal was in sight. Lucia accepted the smallest slice of blueberry linzer torte and then raised her glass, and with a smile in her eye, pointed it toward her father.

"Sing me a song!" she laughed.

The table took up their goblets and pointed toward Leo.

Leo rose to his feet and bowed to everyone. "Before I make a fool of myself, I would just like to thank the Corvinus family for being so kind to my daughter and me and extending such a gracious invitation. Truly we will remember this day for the rest of our lives.

"In my life, I figured I had about as much chance of visiting Lylian as the moon. Which leads me to my favorite song, made famous by Frank Sinatra," Leo set his glass down and then belted out, in his best Sinatra impersonation, "Fly Me to the Moon." At the end of the song everyone stood on their feet and cheered, some steadier than others.

Dessert plates were exchanged with hot and iced coffees for those interested. Lawn chairs were scattered around in the shade of trees, and more than one guest headed to them for a nap. Laszlo and his friends huddled in conversation with the General, while Wan Foo debated with Leo over who was the greater singer, Frank Sinatra or Tony Bennett.

Lucia, Nikita and her two friends walked down to the dock.

"I don't think I can ever eat another thing in my life," Lucia exclaimed. "I am beyond stuffed. I'm storffed!"

"We still have dinner in town," Nikita laughed. "We leave in less than an hour."

"Is it another sit-down dinner like lunch? Nikita, I'm serious, if I eat another thing, I will explode!"

"We won't eat for some time after we get there. It is served buffet-style, so you don't have to worry. Besides, I thought Americans always ate like this."

"Trust me, we don't. Not even on Thanksgiving."

Back near the house, Laszlo and his friends continued to talk with General Rutger.

"Sir, are you quite certain he saw what he claims?" Hannah asked the tall man.

"No we are not," the General admitted. "I'm afraid the man's quite old and not in the best of health mentally. He has said things like this before and been proven wrong. But there is something about his description of the submarine that is just too accurate for him to make up. We have troops in place just to make sure. I'm certain we will find it's just the false ramblings of an old man."

"How could anyone get through the waters without the information in *The Codex?*" Charles asked.

"That is the worrisome thing," the General said.

CHAPTER TWENTY-EIGHT

April 24, 5:21 P.M., Matthias Island, Lylian

THE MERCENARIES WERE FEELING MUCH BETTER.

Once ashore, they had kept to the trees and followed the coastline to a deserted old barn a mile from the landing spot. After a month at sea trapped underwater, it felt good to breathe the open air. Although 10 had died en route, the rest were in perfect shape.

The coyotes had been unloaded and fed. On land the animals were perfectly content and quiet. Part of the Count's training program required outfitting each animal with an electronic collar that shocked them whenever they barked. So by now all the men had to do was put the collars on the coyotes, and that was incentive enough to keep them silent. Unfortunately the submarine had been too much stress for the coyotes, and the threat of a shock hadn't deterred them from howling noisily on board.

Red, satisfied that all was under control, took a satellite phone out of his waterproof backpack and went outside. Protected by trees, he dialed a number. It was answered on the first ring.

"Thirty in good order," he spoke into the phone.

"Excellent," the Count said. He smiled broadly. "Beyond my wildest hopes. Now wait for transportation and keep out of sight."

Red pressed the "End" button and then smashed the phone to pieces, destroying any chance of the phone being traced.

The Count was ecstatic. Thirty men on the island! He would have been happy with even half that. He pressed a speed-dial number for a cell phone in Mauritania. When the phone was answered, the Count spoke. "They have landed. Put your planes in the air now! Head toward Lylian airspace and wait for my signal!"

CHAPTER TWENTY-NINE

April 24, 7:10 P.M., Mathias Island, Lylian

TWO NAVY BLUE LIMOUSINES LEFT THE HOUSE and drove back down the winding mountain road. Leo, Lucia, Nikita, Laszlo and General Rutger rode in one car with Jakob. The other car carried Wan Foo and MeLee with Jakob's brother and his family. The rest of the party was traveling independently.

The window that separated the passenger compartment of the limo was down, and Lucia noticed they had the same driver as before.

"Americans, how was your lunch?" the driver said. "Good, eh?" He laughed as he drove.

"Yes, *they made us a special.*" Lucia said. The whole car roared with laughter.

They crossed from Matthias to Béla Island and over the bridge to Lylian proper. Here the cars slowed to a crawl, the bridge full of people dancing and singing. Groups of nine or ten, arms linked, kicked their legs in formation high into the air.

The driver carefully drove through the crowds and into Corvinus. He drove through the Cliffs neighborhood, choosing alleys and narrow back roads that were less congested with car traffic and people. Lucia noticed the neighborhood change and watched the pavement transform from the Cliffs' pattern of undulating waves to a pattern of white lightning bolts on a background of black. They had entered

Valhalla.

It wasn't just the pavement that was different here. The shops were much tonier and the neighborhood reeked of elegance. The buildings were more uniform in look, and they tried to complement each other rather than stand apart. Clearly, Valhalla was the place to live.

"Not far now," the driver informed his passengers.

The driver pulled over to the side of a small street, full of pedestrian revelers. "You'll need to walk the rest of the way from here, I'm afraid," he said. "I won't be able to drive through the crowds."

"It's not far," Nikita said to Lucia. "Just a couple of blocks."

They all got out of the car, with Lucia, as always, wearing her backpack.

They started down a street of elegant townhomes, crowded with people. Through the blue-lit windows Lucia could see the telltale stacks of goblets and dinner guests enjoying huge banquets, just as she had earlier. Soon they came to a small alley that more closely resembled a long, well-lit tunnel.

"Just down here," Nikita said. They walked toward the noise of even more revelers.

When they came out the other end, Lucia found herself in a large, open square, ringed with restaurants and shops. While similar to the other squares she had seen on the island, this was by far the largest, and the most packed. People filled every restaurant, both inside and out. Milk ran through the streets where people had bumped the bowls set out for cats. Bands played everywhere. Nikita's entourage pushed their way through the throngs until they came to a restaurant right in the center of the square with a large outdoor seating area set with tables and chairs for 50 plus.

"Here we are!" Nikita said. "My father's favorite restaurant and the best on the island."

"Do we have reservations?" Lucia asked.

"Reservations? My father has reserved the entire restaurant. Many more will be joining us here. Lunch was just for close friends."

Hearing she had been included made Lucia very happy.

They entered the restaurant and Nikita and her brother said hello to the *maître d'* and the few guests who had already arrived. Soon the rest of the party joined them to marvel at the madness in the street.

The restaurant was now filling up quickly with the new arrivals. Jakob, Nikita and Laszlo stood at the door and formally greeted everyone. The General stood near the Navigator and regarded everyone who came in very carefully. Katie, Charles, Hannah and Emmett stood close to the door as well and sipped orange sodas.

Lucia and her dad stood outside and watched the wild party in the square from the safety of the cafe.

"Dad, did you know that Nikita's dad reserved the whole restaurant?"

"I'm not surprised. He is a pretty important guy here," he stated matter-of-factly. "I'm just happy he thought of us."

"When do you think the parade happens?" Lucia asked. "And where? There's no way it can come down this street."

"Peanut, relax. We are in good hands. I'm certain it's all taken care of. Let's check out the buffet."

"Eat? Are you kidding? I don't think I'll be able to eat for a month."

Lucia followed her dad over to the buffet table to keep him company.

"Ah, Miss Lucia, are you ready to eat again?" It was Wan Foo and MeLee.

"Oof! No way. Thank you, but I am stuffed. But could you tell me something? Where's the parade, and when do we leave for it?"

"My dear girl, I told you already. The parade comes to us."

Lucia thought for a minute and looked around at the crowd packing the street. Then she looked up and it hit her. *Oh, I am so stupid.* "Of course it comes to us. On the road over our heads!"

CHAPTER THIRTY

April 24, 7:45 P.M., Near Light's End, Lylian

THE SUN WAS SETTING AND THE MEN WERE EDGY. The coyotes were sleeping in one large furry mass.

"Our ride gets here soon," Red said to the men. "Check your gear and put on your game face." They had been checking and rechecking their gear all day to occupy their time and were ready for action.

The men heard a few cars go by during the day, but none had stopped or paid any attention to the decrepit old barn. Now another, larger vehicle came down the road, only this one turned into the drive that led up to their barn hideout. The headlights glared through the boardered-up building, bathing the men inside in speckled light.

The mercenaries pulled out their guns the moment they first heard the truck come up the drive.

The truck stopped outside, and the driver turned the lights off and on in a prearranged code. He got out of the car and approached the building. He didn't knock, but simply stood back and waited.

Red carefully walked out, his men prepared to attack at any sign of danger. Red stared at the figure in front of him, dressed in boots up to his knees and a Cossack's red tunic.

"My name is Sascha. I am looking for men on a Crusade," he said. "I offer transportation."

"That's quite the outfit," Red sneered. "Very subtle." He signaled four of his men to recon the truck.

They examined the truck for anything suspicious and returned to say it was secure. The space would be tight, but it would hold them all. Red told them to load the coyotes. The mercenaries were happy to have something to do and quickly loaded the animals.

"Let's go," Red replied. "I'll ride up front with you."

"Not like that," Sascha said. "If people see you dressed that way they'll know you aren't from here. That could ruin everything. Here, put this on."

Sascha handed Red a blue Cossack's tunic and tall fur hat.

"Now you'll look just like everyone else."

Red resentfully put on the clothes and began to wonder just what kind of country he'd stormed. He sealed the back compartment of the truck and got into the cab.

Satisfied that his passenger would blend in, Sascha got into the truck and backed it out onto the main road.

"How long is the drive to the location?" Red asked.

"Not more than 20 minutes, normally, but this is a holiday, and the streets will be packed with people. We will have to drive slowly."

"What's the holiday, Halloween?" Red said. He tugged on his fur hat.

"I don't think you would understand," Sascha said. He kept his eyes on the road, stopping any further conversation. The foreigner was irritating, he thought. But he would do anything to help the Crusade. Very soon, his days of waiting on tables at the *Café Kék Macska* would be over.

They continued down the road following the coastline. In the distance the blue glow of Light's End came into view. The truck kept to the outer edge of the town, and though traffic was busy, they made good time. Red stared out the window at the show passing by.

"Are you sure it ain't Halloween, 'cause it looks like a costume party out there," he said.

"You would do well to keep your thoughts to yourself," Sascha cautioned. "Lylians are easygoing but very proud of their country and their culture."

Red thought to say something else. The unbalanced look in the driver's eyes him made him decide otherwise.

They had passed through town and were leaving the outskirts.

"It's just up the road," Sascha said. "We're almost there."

Red looked around nervously as the truck took a right off the main road and drove up a windy dirt road to the edge of the island. They pulled up to an old building in ruins, about five stories tall, that clearly had been much larger before it crumbled. It was round at the base, and as it rose, it narrowed to a conical shape.

"What is this place?" he asked.

"It is the remains of an ancient lighthouse from the time before."

"What do you mean 'the time before'?"

"I mean it is from the time before. It is older than the pyramids. No one comes here. You will be safe for the night."

The wind howled through the ruins, and far below, Red could hear the waves crashing against the steep cliffs.

"I'll be glad when this job is over," Red muttered.

"This is as close as we can get you to the airport and keep you undetected," Sascha said. "I will drive you to the planned attack point before sunrise. I suggest you unload your men and let them rest. We will be here only a few hours."

Red didn't like taking orders, especially from someone dressed like a hotel doorman, but he held his tongue and opened the back of the truck. The men and coyotes were happy to get out into the fresh air.

Red and the driver walked through the huge doorway and looked around. Inside the building it looked even more cavernous. It was one enormous open room, like a cathedral, with a few smaller rooms around the perimeters, like little offices. A ceiling five stories above them had partially collapsed. With the night sky visible and the moon shining, it was light enough to make out some details. The walls were massively thick, cut from large chunks of stone. Filthy with age, the stones had once been a checkerboard of white and black, though they were now mostly a dingy gray. Around the perimeter of the wall a staircase spiraled up and through the open ceiling overhead. In the center of the room, a broad staircase led down several floors.

"We will sleep down there," Sascha said. He pointed down the stairwell. "There are several sub-levels, so you can put those animals on a floor below you. We've set up a generator for lights, and we won't get wet if it rains. Warn your men that a few more will be joining us. And tell them to put away their weapons. I don't want anyone to get hurt."

Red relayed the information. "Get some sleep: Show time is at 0400 hours," he said.

"Sleep?" one of the soldiers complained. "That's all we've been doing for a month. I want a little action."

"You'll get it soon enough. Now do as you're told. Post four men outside on the perimeter. We'll do two-hour shifts. Be careful what you shoot at; we're expecting a few more islanders. The rest of you stow your weapons."

"Should we bring a couple coyotes?" one of the men asked.

"No, I don't want them ignoring their collars and howling at the moon."

CHAPTER THIRTY-ONE

April 24, 8:19 P.M., Corvinus, Lylian

THE RESTAURANT WAS NOW FILLED WITH REVELERS. Nikita was excused from greeting duty and joined Lucia, talking with Viktoria and Stephan, the threesome having cemented their friendship after the initial wariness. They had staked out a table right on the edge of the plaza with a perfect view for the parade.

"My dad makes these things so formal sometimes," Nikita said. "Lucia, are you hungry at all?"

Lucia winced and changed the subject. "Nikita, I wonder if we'll see Aranck?"

"Perhaps. The parade shouldn't be much longer now."

"How do you know when it's going to start? I don't want to miss any of it."

"You won't. I can assure you of that," Nikita said. Then as if to underscore her words, the sky suddenly exploded into a sea of blue fireworks filling the air. People were cheering everywhere.

As the fireworks faded from view, the crowds became very silent and all eyes looked overhead. The anticipation was huge, and no one moved. Then off in the distance where people were massed a block or two away, Lucia could hear applause.

"They are very near," Nikita whispered.

Lucia saw people looking left, so she did the same. The square was already well lit, and in anticipation of the parade, lights had been hung to illuminate the catwalks, too. At a far edge of the square, people started clapping. Lucia saw movement overhead. Coming toward her were young yet very ordinary cats running along the catwalk. They were moving extremely fast, however, so people applauded nonetheless.

"I thought it might be a bit more," Lucia said.

"They're running ahead of the parade to check the route," Nikita said. "Just wait."

A few minutes later, from across town, crowds started clapping again. This time there was no mistaking that something big headed their way. The sound grew louder and stronger until around the corner and into the square came a thundering herd of thousands of cats. Atop each cat sat a Lytle on a leather saddle, the reins in one hand and a sword wielded in the other.

The sound created was amazing. Thousands of cat paws hitting the stone and wood paths in a million soft thuds, the sound of leather rubbing against fur, and the squeaking of leather against leather. As they rode along, the Lytles would softly dig their heels into the cats, causing them to yowl in time to some ancient rhythm. You could see the cats enjoyed the strange sounds they created in songs as old as the island.

As the cats yowled, the Lytles accompanied them in a strange sort of yodeling counterpoint. The Lytles on occasion would scrape their swords against the buildings, sending sparks flying and adding more sounds into the cool night air.

"Do you like?" Nikita asked.

Lucia could not answer or take her eyes off the spectacle. She was spellbound. She was not alone, for all across the plaza, people sat mesmerized at some spectacular feat of skill performed, or they

153

pointed excitedly at a particularly well-outfitted rider and cat.

The skill of the riders was beyond anything Lucia had ever seen. They rode fast and furiously. Some leaned forward in their saddles as their cats galloped at top speed. Others stood on their saddles, swords scraping in time to the music. Still others rode as if they had come from some Wild West rodeo. They jumped from one side to the other on their cats, holding onto the saddles as the cats raced along.

Now, a thousand cats or more circled the square a story above the crowd. They had slowed down from the frenetic pace of their arrival and now simply circled the square, catching their breath. A signal was given and the circling stopped. The cats sat back on their haunches, and the riders, still astride, looked down to the audience below. All flick swords were pointed out and down at the crowd.

Another signal sounded, and in unison, each rider raised his sword to the night sky and closed it, creating a thunderous shower of clicks that echoed off the square's stone walls. The riders dismounted, herded their cats to the side and then perched on the narrow ledges with their feet dangling off the edge. The Lytles talked among themselves, a few acknowledging their admirers below.

"What happens now?" Lucia asked.

"Now the show begins," Nikita answered. "They perform different feats that show off their riding ability, swordsmanship and bravery. It's the same display they put on when my ancestors first settled here over 400 years ago."

Lucia looked across the square and watched waiters from the restaurants, along with many of the crowd, joining together to carry out large sections of scaffolding with crossbeams at different heights. The sections, several stories tall, weren't connected to each other but were scattered throughout the entire square 10 and 20 feet apart.

"It looks like a giant jungle gym," Lucia said.

"I don't know what that is, but I will take your word for it. This portion of the parade takes place all over the town. Each area makes its own *állvány*, or scaffolding. It is a great honor to work on the construction crew. Some of these scaffolds are very simple, while others can be very ornate. I think ours is a nice balance. The important thing is that it be very solid, so as to not tip over, and varied in design, so the riders are put to the test.

"They're going to ride on those boards? They're barely as wide as a cat."

"That is part of the skill," Nikita said. "Now enjoy the show."

Four waiters carried out the final component, which was a large stage about seven feet tall. Once the stage was fixed in place, several dozen Lytles from around the square made their way to it.

The crowd noise died down as the Lytles talked quietly among themselves, casually scratching their cats under the chin.

With a cry, one of the Lytles leapt onto his cat and took off across the stage, jumped onto the nearest scaffold, and shot across it as fast as he could. As he neared the end of the board, he bounded up and over to the next scaffold and continued his run. Now another Lytle leapt onto a cat and took off in a different direction, leaping to another scaffold. Soon their were dozens and then hundreds of cats running in every direction from scaffold to scaffold, racing up and down, from the top-most ledge and back down to street level.

The Lytles were whooping and yelling and urging their cats into even more dangerous stunts. Riders charged each other, swords drawn, and at the last conceivable moment one would dive over the other to avoid crashing. This went on for 30 minutes with tired performers replaced by fresh ones that carried on the same fevered pace.

Some riders carried large grapes with them and flung them in to the air so another rider could slice them in half, at full gallop, the two pieces falling to the crowd below who eagerly jostled for the pieces to pop in their mouth.

"Boy, they sure want to get a piece of grape," Lucia said.

"It is a superstition here," Nikita replied. "If you eat one of the grapes you will have good luck for the rest of the year."

"Then get me a grape!" Lucia cried and leaned forward in hopes of catching one.

Finally, most of the Lytles in the square had run the course. After letting their cats enjoy the saucers of milk scattered around the square, they returned to the catwalk and waited for the next exhibition.

"That was awesome!" Lucia exclaimed.

"There is still more to come," Nikita said.

The girls watched as men carried out several dozen round table tops, about five feet in diameter, and attached them with bolts to the *állvány* standing at different heights all across the square. Lucia stared intently. In anticipation of what, she did not know.

"Be patient, Lucia," Nikita said as the men finished attaching the small stages. "You will like this."

With their task complete, the men melted back into the crowd and the entire square grew silent.

When Lucia's eyes returned to the Lytles above, she saw that all of them were now standing at attention, while their cats were relaxing and licking themselves. The Lytles suddenly raised their right arm high over their heads, and with a thunderous yell started running along the ledge, gaining speed as they went. They ran maybe 20 feet, and with another thunderous roar, leapt from the ledge and out onto the *állvány*, vaulting themselves with effortless ease as each group raced to a predetermined round stage.

Lucia looked around at the Corvinus guests, who awaited the

Lytles' next feat in nervous anticipation.

The Lytles formed into groups of seven, standing in loose circles. Then, as one, these hundreds of gathered Lytles let out an enormous shout, drew their flick swords and opened them high into the night air. The groups of seven each lunged forward striking at the air in a series of long-practiced moves. They twirled around and stabbed at the air again and again. Without warning or discussion, they would all—as one—feign sword strikes in one direction and then another. And each group of seven had its own distinct style.

"It's beautiful and powerful," Lucia said. "But what are they doing?"

"They are defending themselves from assailants," Nikita said. She never took her eyes away from the exhibition. "A team of seven Lytles is a basic fighting unit. They practice for years and years with the same group, perfecting their skills so they act as one. Each unit works like a wheel, and when you put a hundred wheels together, they are unstoppable!"

The Lytles continued their demonstration, with the noise of the swords and the stomp of their feet creating a sound all its own. The exhibition went on for several more minutes until, with a final shout and lunge of the sword, it was over. At least that's what Lucia thought.

She again observed the crowd, assuming they would start to clap and refill their glasses. But none of them moved. Instead she could hear an excited murmur race through it. Rather than ask any more questions, she watched the spot where everyone else was looking. She didn't have to wait long.

Lucia followed everyone's gaze toward the center of the square, where she noticed a large wooden pole. It reminded her of a barbershop pole. Next to it stood a lone Lytle holding his sword. He looked around the square, and once satisfied with what he saw, struck his sword against a piece of stone or flint attached to the pole, and in an instant, the whole thing lit up in flames.

With a huge cry the throng of Lytles who had remained on the building ledges hoisted their flick swords and ran forward, launching themselves off the ledge and through the air to land on the *állvány*. Thousands of Lytles charged toward the waiting groups of seven.

At first the fighting groups remained motionless, their swords hanging at their sides. As the mob of Lytles drew near, the sevens sprang into action. They drew their swords as one and flicked them to full length. Metal clashed on metal as they defended themselves from their brethren. As their swords sliced through the air, steel on steel, sparks flew, creating flashes of light that filled the square. Again and again, the Lytles raced toward the sevens trying to pierce their lines of defense. Every time, they were turned away. Lucia could not imagine how anyone—or anything—could defend themselves against such an overwhelming assault. But they did, again and again.

The log, which had been burning since the first attack, was now almost extinguished. The Lytle who had set the fire that started the onslaught now drew his sword once more, and with a mighty swing, cut the pole down at its base, signaling that the fighting was over.

The crowd went wild with applause and cheers as thousands of cats jumped down and into the square, each to retrieve a Lytle. The cats raced by, never breaking pace, as Lytles jumped on their back to be whisked away. In a matter of moments, the entire square was clear of Lytles, who were now all safely back at roof level.

"Do you see why my forefathers never took up arms against them, so long ago?" Nikita asked Lucia.

Lucia could only nod in agreement.

"What are they going to do now?" Lucia asked. She watched the dozen riders gathering on the stage. "What could possibly top that?"

"This is the Medallion Run. See at the top of that building, the Chinese pagoda? There are small blue medallions hanging from leather lanyards. They race up the side of the building to grab their medallion and back down again. The first one down gets to keep the medallion," Nikita said.

The competition began and the crowd quietly watched the riders race up the side of the building in pursuit of the blue medallion. Claws dug into the wood siding of the pagoda as the cats climbed their way to the top. The riders were bunched together so tightly you could not tell who might reach the prize first.

Staring fixedly at the ascending riders, Lucia shouted out, "That's Aranck. He's riding Bátor right up the side of that building."

With only yards to go, Aranck edged ahead. As he rode straight up he drew out his flick sword, opened it and snatched one of the blue medallions. He slung it over his neck, turned Bátor around and rode straight back down the side of the building. He jumped the last 10 feet to land back onto the raised stage in the center of the plaza. Aranck held the medallion up for all to see.

The people sitting jumped to their feet and those standing raised their arms in one gigantic cheer.

Using this opportunity to clear dishes, a busy waiter carrying a heavily laden tray was passing the table where Lucia sat immersed in the festival. The sudden roar of the crowd startled him—and losing his balance—the heavy tray slipped from his hands and crashed into Lucia's back, pushing her forward into the table, knocking her down. The waiter was mortified and quickly grabbed a towel to clean her off.

Lucia looked around to see a swarm of heads all going in and out of focus.

"Did a cat fall on me?" she asked. The face in front of her was blurry.

"Lucia, are you all right?" Nikita asked. She seemed a hundred miles away.

Leo leaned over his daughter, who was covered in cold spaghetti.

"Lucia, how many fingers am I holding up?"

"Thursday?" she answered. "Dad, I'm just kidding. Three fingers, okay? But, geez, I'm a mess."

"I think we better get you back to the hotel," Leo said. He looked around for his host to say goodnight.

"Dad, I'll be fine" Lucia said. "I'm just covered in food. Really, I want to stay and see the rest of the circus."

"I think you've had enough excitement for the night, Peanut."

"Lucia, Laszlo and I can take you back in the car," Nikita said. "Besides, the festival is almost over. Mr. Boyd, please stay to see the end. My father would be disappointed if you left. Lucia is my guest, and I will see her safely home. We'll send the limo back for you."

Leo thought about it while he looked at his daughter. He looked to Jakob who assured him his daughter would be well taken care of and implored Leo to stay for the rest of the festival.

"Really, Dad, I'll be fine with Nikita," Lucia said. "I'd hate for you to miss out just because of me."

"Alright, but I'll be back shortly. Go up to the room, put a cold, wet washcloth on your forehead and lie down."

Lucia kissed her dad goodnight and walked off with Nikita and Laszlo.

CHAPTER THIRTY-TWO

April 24, 11:12 P.M., Corvinus, Lylian

LUCIA WALKED IN A DAZE BACK TO THE CAR with Nikita and Laszlo. The evening had been more amazing than she ever could have expected. To think that just a few weeks ago a big deal was breakfast at the Egg and I back in Minneapolis and now she was watching a spectacle that few—outside of Lylian—had ever seen. Her head ached and she was covered in food, but it had been the best day of her life. All the last few days had been the best days of her life.

The three retraced their steps back to the car, Nikita and Laszlo each holding one of Lucia's arms to support her. The car was parked where they had left it. They looked around and saw the driver standing in the shadows of an alley, smoking a cigarette. He gave them a brief wave.

"Are you ready to go?" To Lucia, his voice sounded somehow different than before. "Where are the others?"

"It will be just the three of us," Laszlo said. Without waiting for the driver to open the doors, Laszlo helped Lucia into the limo. "Mr. Boyd will be riding with my father. Now if you will hurry, this girl has been injured."

The driver finished his cigarette and walked slowly back to the car. He paused for a minute beside the car and looked around as if uncertain what to do. He thought a minute more then shrugged his shoulders and got in. He slowly pulled the car away from the curb, avoiding the few people walking the backstreets.

"Take us to the hotel directly," Laszlo said.

After a while he caught the driver's reflection in the rearview mirror and didn't like what he saw. "Excuse me, but you're not our driver. What's going on? Who are you?"

"His, uh, wife was taken ill," the driver said. "Just sit back; we're almost there."

The driver pressed a button and the privacy glass between him and the passengers started rising.

"Wife?" Laszlo said. "He doesn't have a wife!"

Lucia didn't understand what was going on, but from Laszlo's reaction, she knew something was not right. She watched him press the control to lower the window, but it wasn't working.

"Nikita, try the doors!" Lucia cried, but to no avail. They would not budge; the locks were jammed.

As the compartment sealed shut, Lucia heard a hissing sound and smelled a funny odor. Immediately she began feeling light-headed as some sort of gas poured in. She turned to look at Nikita and Lazlo, who were already feeling the same effect. Moments later the three passed out, with Lucia slumping over her backpack.

The driver drove slowly through the crowded streets, just one more limo on the road carrying Cat Festival partiers. The darkened windows hid the unconscious bodies in back.

The driver was ecstatic. He had the American girl and the backpack! Plus he had the Navigator's two offspring. This could all be turned to their advantage. But first he must get to the others.

He crossed from Valhalla into the Moorland district and finally across Shepard's Bridge and out of Corvinus. Once on the other side of the Crescent River, the traffic became noticeably quieter. He drove as fast as he dared on the narrow, tight-curved road, traveling due north. Leaving the main route, he turned left and followed an old logging trail up to a high ledge surrounded by trees.

He stopped the car 200 yards beyond a pre-designated mile marker and got out. Instinctively he looked around to see if he was being watched. It was late at night in the middle of nowhere; there was no chance of being spotted by anyone, he reassured himself. He walked over to the side of the road and cleared the brush off a small rutted path. He drove the car up the path and stopped at the steep mountain wall. From the mountainside he removed more cut branches to reveal a cave.

Hidden in the cave was a small van with keys in the ignition. He started it and pulled up next to the car. Then, assuring himself again that he would be undetected, he transferred the unconscious passengers from the limo into the back of the van. He was confident his prisoners would not wake for hours. Once the switch had been accomplished, he parked the limo in the cave, reusing the brush to cover the entrance.

Satisfied the trail was obscured from view, he drove back down the mountain toward Light's End, feeling considerably safer now that he had ditched the limo for the nondescript van.

My cousin will reward me handsomely, the driver thought. He wondered, as he had many times before, just how generous the Count would be.

Observing from a ledge high above the kidnapper's secret cave, three Lytles watched. The distance had been far too great for them to arrive in time to stop the crime, but that did not deter them long.

"I know their destination," Rowtag said. "But we need more

Lytles. To The Tilt!"

"*The Tilt!*" cried Nosh and Chepi and turned their cats toward home.

CHAPTER THIRTY-THREE

April 25, 12:20 A.M., The Tilt, Lylian

AFTER THE CAT FESTIVAL, THE LYTLES HAD RETURNED home to The Tilt. Most sailed back across Matthias Lake, while others rode all the way home on thread-like concealed trails. A few hundred remained, discussing the evening's parade and how much fun it had been, while waiting on shore for empty boats to return. Young Lytles fell asleep, nestled in the fur of slumbering cats.

Unexpectedly from the darkness, Rowtag, Nosh and Chepi galloped in, having ridden hard and fast from the kidnapping scene. Jumping from his cat, Rowtag shouted to several of the Lytles nearest him.

"The Banished have the serum!"

"How is that possible?" Aranck asked. He was tall for a Lytle, standing over 10 inches head to toe. At that height he towered over his family and most of the thousands of other Lytles. But Aranck never felt as small as he did now.

Heaving a saddle from a small wooden stand in the stable, Aranck reached up and placed it on the back of Bátor. He strapped it firmly on, all the while thinking about only one thing: The Lytles were dying.

Introduced into the Lytle population almost 50 years ago and growing in strength, the virus was now ready to fulfill its lethal task.

165

This Lytle generation would be the last—not one of them destined to live beyond their teenage years. As they matured, their lungs would slowly fail until they could breathe no more.

Aranck's own children were sick with the disease as well. Thankfully they didn't know of their fatal condition. Nor did every Lytle know the importance of the American girl's invention. Those Lytles who did were quickly horrified to think it had fallen into enemy hands.

Rowtag quickly explained the situation and the kidnappings.

"If they cause the girl any harm, they will have to answer to me!" Aranck said.

"You will have your chance to save her, Aranck," Rowtag said, "I'm certain they are heading for Light's End."

"We need to move fast," Aranck said.

"We'll take two teams—14 of us should be more then enough—we can move faster than taking a whole army," Rowtag said. He quickly sized up those nearby and selected seven Epps and six Meks to accompany him on the journey, including Chepi, Nosh and Alawa.

Aranck was already saddling up Bátor, preparing for battle. The 14 mounted their cats and entered a nearby boat storage cave.

Holding torches for illumination, Rowtag led the way down a narrow path to the back of the cave. The ledge opened up to a broad, flat floor. In the center was a large circular cage of metal suspended several inches off the floor by cables hanging from the ceiling. Underneath was a large metal platform ornately decorated in ancient patterns.

Aranck and six others rode their cats into the cage.

Chepi walked over to a small metal plate on the wall and rotated it to reveal a small opening the size of her fist. She stepped back and drew her flick sword to its full length and jammed it all the way into the opening. There was a quiet click and the metal platform under the cage divided in the center, revealing a deep shaft. The cage began to slowly descend into it, dropping steadily for a full 10 minutes.

The shaft they traveled down had a smooth, polished surface carved with etchings and lit by the faint glow of quartz rocks evenly placed along the walls. The quartz gave off a natural, phosphorescent light, illuminating their descent. When they reached the bottom, the Lytles got out and the cage began its journey back up the shaft. Once it returned to the surface, Chepi and the remaining six Lytles got in the cage and began their descent to join the others.

The Lytles regrouped in a large room with a high barrel-vault ceiling. Eons ago its walls had been flattened smooth and carved into elaborate pillars, etched with scenes of historic battles and figures. There were even more quartz rocks used in these walls, giving the space a soft glow. At the end of the room were two circular openings, opposite each other, in the facing walls. Connecting them was a curved pipe. Sitting on the pipe were Lytle cable cars.

This was an underground train station.

The Lytles quickly loaded the cats into cars and crammed themselves into the front one. They closed the roof, and Alawa activated the cable clutch. The car lurched forward with a sharp jump. She adjusted quickly and they were soon flying along smoothly.

This underground cable system was rarely used. It was initially built as a fast way for the Lytles to travel to the Light's End side of the island. Light's End had once been a busy and important hub on the island, and long ago it served humans and Lytles alike. But since the Great Catastrophe there was little need to visit; Light's End's important purpose and significance had been lost over the ages. Yet, the system was still in working order.

The warriors moved swiftly underground, covering the 10-mile distance in less than 30 minutes. Reaching their destination, Alawa released the cable clutcher and diverted them to a sidetrack.

They disembarked and, mounting their cats, rode toward a large metal door of polished copper engraved with symbols of a starry sky with planets and moons, like a planetarium ceiling. Chepi drew her flick sword and again pushed it to the hilt into a small depression in the wall. The copper door opened, revealing a set of stairs. They had arrived at Light's End station, eight levels below the surface.

"Zurzavar Hoz Ellenség!" The Lytles whispered as they headed up the stairs, and up to battle.

CHAPTER THIRTY-FOUR

April 25, 12:45 A.M., Corvinus, Lylian

THE RESTAURANT HOSTING JAKOB'S PARTY was now almost empty, with just a few stragglers enjoying one last bite of food.

Leo waited with Jakob and General Rutger for the car to return so they could drive home. He was concerned about the bump his daughter received and was starting to feel a bit guilty *(a lot guilty)* about letting her go home without him.

"Where is that car? Jakob said. "He never keeps me waiting. Come, gentlemen, let's walk up to the road. Perhaps he's waiting for us there."

The three said goodnight to the lingering guests and went in search of the limo. Emmett, Hannah, Charles and Katie walked along with them.

Retracing their steps through the alley tunnel, they reached the street and found it deserted.

"This is odd," Jakob said. "They've been gone over an hour."

Leo wondered if Lucia had been hurt worse than he thought and Nikita and Laszlo had taken her to a hospital.

Everyone began to suspect that all was not as it was supposed to be when Hannah, who had wandered up the street to check around, heard a soft moan coming from a cul-de-sac. Silently, she signaled the others, who joined her.

"Charles, come with me," the General whispered. "The rest of you, on your toes."

Hannah, Katie and Emmett stood guard, putting Leo and Jakob between them and the wall while General Rutger and Charles entered the cul-de-sac. Everyone, except Leo and Jakob, held a weapon in their hand.

General Rutger had carried a small flashlight with him that he shone down the alley as he and Charles moved in. Their eyes swept back and forth, Charles concentrating on the right side and Rutger on the left. The alleyway was narrow, and the few doors they tested as they passed were all locked. As they cautiously moved in, both saw a leg stir behind several garbage cans. The General signaled Charles to move them as he stood ready for action.

Charles lifted the empty garbage container with one swift move, exposing a man lying on his stomach, his head covered in blood. He let out another soft moan. It was the limo driver.

"Navigator! It's your driver!" General Rutger said urgently. "Here, Charles, help me lift him up. Gently! Gently!"

They helped the man to his feet. Clotted blood had dried on his face and there was a nasty gash across his forehead.

"My God, man, are you alright?" Jakob spoke quickly to the driver. "What happened? Where are the girls? Where's Laszlo? Where's the car?"

"I … I don't know," the man said, his voice foggy. "I parked the car here and was going to join friends to watch the parade. I got out to lock the car when behind me a voice asked if I had a match. I remember my hands going into my pockets to help him out, and the next thing I know … I'm talking to you."

"So you never saw the parade!" the General said. "That means whoever hit you has had the car for hours."

"But Lucia, Nikita, Laszlo, they would have come back saying the car was gone!" Leo said, dread taking over his voice.

"I don't think the car was gone when they got here," General Rutger said. "I think the thief's intent was to commandeer whomever was riding in that car."

"But that would have been you, me and Jakob as well!" Leo said. "Jakob, they have our children!"

The group stood there silently taking in all that had just happened.

Suddenly Leo cried out, "My God, they also have Lucia's backpack! They have her invention! *They have her serum!*"

The General clapped his hands once. "That's the first piece of good news I've heard."

"How can that be good news?" Jakob asked.

"Because I had Laszlo place a tracking device in it on the plane ride over from Budapest," General Rutger replied.

"I don't understand," Leo said. "Lucia met Nikita on the plane by accident. They just started talking about the island …"

General Rutger cut Leo off mid-sentence. "Sorry to be so mysterious, Mr. Boyd, but her serum will make a far greater impact on our nation than you could ever imagine. Our agents have been following you—protecting you and your family—for months now."

"But they have the backpack …" Leo said.

"They have it, but not for long. You four, did you ride your bikes here?"

"Sir, yes sir, they're just over there," Hannah said, pointing down the street.

"Use your GPS transponders to follow this signal." The General handed them a number to input into their tracking systems.

The four saluted and ran down the narrow street. Parked in its shadows sat four black Ducati Streetfighter motorcycles. They started the bikes and each punched up a small touch screen and input the numbers given them by the General. They waited for the system to link with a navigation satellite 240 miles overhead. The system paused, then the bike monitors showed a green-blinking ping.

"Light's End!" Katie said. They took off down the street, squealing away, their front tires high in the air.

Leo stared in bafflement. "But who are they?" he asked.

"They work for me. They're Lylian Black Army Rangers," General Rutger said.

"But there's just four of them. What can they possibly do?"

"They're Black Army. They can do anything!"

CHAPTER THIRTY-FIVE

April 25, 12:55 A.M., Lights End, Lylian

THE KIDNAPPER PULLED TO A STOP at the ruins at Light's End.

Two men approached the van as two more watched in the shadows with weapons drawn. "I believe you are expecting me," the kidnapper said. "I have three unconscious bodies in the back that need to be moved quickly." The guards opened the side door and saw the stilled bodies. After ensuring there would be no surprises, one of the guards went inside to get help moving the prisoners.

"What are we doing with a child?" the remaining guard asked. He hoisted Lucia up over his shoulder like a garment bag.

"Careful with all of them," the kidnapper said. "They are valuable to our mission."

Sascha came out with Red and the others and spoke to the kidnapper in Lylianese. The conversation was rapid and angry.

"Hey, what are you two talking about?" Red demanded.

"My associate was to bring several others to join us, and he has failed," Sascha said.

"I did my best," the kidnapper said. He held up the backpack. "Besides, we have this."

Red pointed at Laszlo. "Put him in a cell on one of the lower levels," he said. "The girls will stay with us."

Two men, each holding one of his arms, dragged Laszlo three

floors down to a small holding cell. The ancient wooden door was in disrepair, but the mercenaries devised a way to lock it.

"At least this one isn't dressed like a circus clown," one of Lazlos's captors said.

"I think my old Aunt Minnie could have taken this island with her crochet hook," another said. They all laughed at their prisoner.

They searched Laszlo for weapons and took his wallet, penknife and smartphone.

"My music?" Laszlo said. His voice was groggy, perhaps a little intentionally.

"Let him have his music," a guard said. "There's no phone signal down here and it'll keep him occupied." The other tossed Laszlo the smartphone. "But don't get too comfortable, we'll be back for you shortly."

Laszlo said nothing but sat back on the bunk, arms folded across his chest. For the first time since the kidnapping, Laszlo smiled.

Chapter Thirty-Six

April 25, 1:23 A.M., Corvinus, Lylian

THE FOUR MOTORCYCLES TORE THROUGH CORVINUS and across the Eight Man Bridge. They checked their GPS screens to ensure the signal hadn't moved—or worse—been detected and destroyed. The wind was cool against their faces as they flew down the road, hugging the turns, the bikes drafting each other to cut down on wind resistance.

"The signal is just south of town," Hannah spoke into her throat mike. "It has to be the old tower."

"We'll be there shortly. Emmett, what's your plan?" Charles asked.

"Here's what we'll do," Emmett said. He proceeded to lay out a plan of attack as they sped toward the tower on the treacherous roads.

They arrived at Light's End a short time later. Their first stop was the bookstore. Despite the late hour, Porthos was still up and greeted them warmly.

"To what do I owe this unexpected, but nonetheless welcome, visit? he asked. "I'm afraid Anne has already gone to bed. She will be disappointed to hear her favorite grandchild—and her friends—stopped by on Cat Festival and she was asleep."

"Granddad—*Major*—this is business." Katie said. The group quickly explained the situation.

"I knew something was happening," Porthos said. He slammed his fist into the palm of his hand. "The Boyds came here by happenstance just yesterday. I brought them back to Corvinus myself. I told General Rutger all about it."

"We believe they're in the tower, and we need you to help us get as close as possible without being detected," Emmett said. "Our motorcycles are simply too noisy and suspicious-looking."

"You are all familiar with the tower?" Porthos asked.

"*Granddad*, we've only been playing in it all our lives," Katie said. "What about more Rangers?"

"Far too risky, sir," Emmett explained. "If we go in with a huge force, the kidnappers might kill the hostages before we could overpower them."

Porthos thought for a moment. "I have an old rowboat. It will be tight, but it is quiet and there is a stream that runs very near the tower."

"That will work," Emmett said. "Drop two of us on the near side and two on the far side. Let's move."

The Rangers grabbed night-vision goggles and Tasers from their bikes and crammed into Porthos' small boat. They quietly and quickly rowed the tiny boat down the darkly lit stream, and a few minutes later Hannah and Emmett had climbed the embankment into the trees surrounding the tower's steep hill.

The boat continued downstream to the spot where Katie and Charles would also make their way to the protection of the woods. All four Rangers moved slowly up the steep mountainside in pairs, alert for danger.

After climbing silently for 15 minutes, Hannah broke the silence and whispered into her mic, "There are two men at the tower entrance. From what I can tell, they seem more bored than on guard.

They do have night-vision goggles, so be discreet."

"Hannah, I'll circle to the other side," Emmett whispered. "We'll need to be close to use our Tasers on them."

Katie and Charles found the other two guards crouched by the truck, sharing a cigarette. Katie whispered, "Hannah, Emmett, we're in position to take out our two."

"All, on my mark," Hannah commanded. "Three ... two ... one ... fire!"

An instant later, 50,000 volts of electricity were delivered to the four soldiers, rendering them helpless. The Rangers quickly tied them up and gagged them.

The moment the guards left him in the cell, Laszlo popped in his earbuds and activated a hidden menu on his smartphone. "May Day! This is Army Ranger Laszlo Corvinus. Do you read me?"

"Laszlo, it's me!" Charles whispered into his throat mic. "Where are you? Are you all right?"

"I'm in the Light's End tower. It looks like I'm three or four levels down. I'm fine. Nikita, Lucia and I were kidnapped just after the parade. I stupidly let myself get caught. Grab the team and get here now."

"We're right outside ... the four of us."

"There are three men guarding me. I'll disable them and create a diversion down here. There are at least a couple dozen, perhaps more. I saw a couple of Lylians as well. I have no idea where the girls are. Stay alert," he said, breaking contact with the Ranger.

Laszlo settled back on the floor in the corner of the small cell. The hallway outside was dimly lit. Laszlo could hear several men approaching. They unlocked the cell. A bearded man and another guard holding a gun entered. "Come with us and no trouble," the bearded man snarled.

Laszlo rose from the floor, holding his smartphone, "But I'm afraid I must make a little trouble," he said smiling. He pressed a button on his smartphone and the case snapped open. Concealed inside was a Lytle flick sword. The guard reacted to the movement and raised his weapon. Laszlo was much quicker. With a sharp snap of his wrist he extended the blade to its full six feet, locking it in place and piercing the armed guard's heart with one motion. The guard fell dead.

Laszlo quickly pressed the blade's release button and flicked it downward to long knife length, then jumped forward and extended his weapon against the neck of the bearded man, slightly breaking the skin with the deadly sharp blade.

"Now if you would be so kind as to tell me where my sister and our American friend are being held, I might spare your life," Laszlo said.

The bearded man told him everything. Laszlo tied the guard up with his own rope and gagged him so he could not cry out. He removed the firing pin from the gun. He felt much more comfortable using his flick sword, and to his advantage, these intruders had no idea what the sword could do. All the better, he thought.

No Lylian really knew the tower's original purpose. That it was a lighthouse of some sort was obvious to anyone. But it was certainly much more than that. While this wonderful old structure would be one of the Seven Wonders of the Ancient World almost anywhere else, and a top tourist attraction for any country, the Lylians left it and the island's past right where it was—in the past.

But now the building was playing a very definite role in Lylian's future.

Laszlo crept out into the dark hallway. His prisoner had told him the third guard would be in the larger room down the hall and to the left. As he approached the room he could see the beam of a powerful flashlight spilling into the hallway. Carefully, he turned the corner of the hallway and edged toward the light. The guard was kneeling on the floor with his back to the door, going through his gear.

He heard a movement behind him and turned to see the Black Army Ranger. He yelled out for backup, sprang to his feet and kicked his foot sharply into Lazlo's midsection, knocking him back. He spun around and kicked out his feet and hands in a flurry of martial arts kicks and punches.

Laszlo quickly caught his balance and started fending off the lethal blows.

Pushing him against the wall, the mercenary pulled out a knife and lunged at Laszlo's chest. Laszlo ducked to the side, the knife hitting the wall and breaking in half. He grabbed the man and knocked his head into the wall. He fell motionless to the floor, the broken knife slipping from his hand.

Laszlo nimbly secured the man with rope from the guard's own backpack and gagged him as well. Luckily, the thick walls had muffled the man's cry for backup. Now Laszlo just needed to figure out how to draw some of the other invaders downstairs without getting himself killed.

Hearing movement behind him, he spun around to face the door and, looking down, got his answer.

"Rowtag, Aranck," Laszlo said. "I should have counted on you showing up."

CHAPTER THIRTY-SEVEN

April 25, 2:18 A.M., Lights End, Lylian

LUCIA AND NIKITA SLOWLY CAME TO on the damp stone floor, the cold sea air reviving them.

"Mmmph," Lucia said groggily. "What happened? Where … where are we?"

The girls sat up and looked around. They were in a room, half the size of a tennis court, surrounded by more than a dozen men, armed and looking very dangerous. One of the men tossed them a water bottle.

"Drink some water; it will help clear your head," he said gruffly.

The girls shared the bottle and looked around warily at the soldiers.

Nikita spoke to the men. "Release us immediately. Do you know who I am? You harm one hair on my head, and you'll be in a world of trouble."

One of the soldiers walked over to her and yanked her up by her hair.

"What, with this blue hair? Who's going to come save you?" He laughed and tossed her back down on the ground.

"You leave her alone!" Lucia said, kicking the soldier in the shin.

He howled with pain and backhanded her across the face, knocking Lucia down, where she landed on her ribs. Lucia writhed on the floor in pain, the defiance she showed earlier turning to fear.

"Stop it," Red screamed. He knocked the soldier down with his fist. "One more outta line act like that—from any man—and he goes home in a body bag!"

Lucia fought back tears as she laid her head in Nikita's lap.

"Where's my brother?" Nikita asked.

"He's down below. Now what's this about?" Red reached for Lucia's backpack by his feet.

"I don't know what you're talking about," Lucia said. She forgot about the pain in her side and tried to think of how she could protect her serum. In despair, she realized there was little she and Nikita could do.

"Little girl, I don't have much time. We're leaving here in less than two hours, and I need to know what is so important about whatever's in this bag. Let's just have a look."

Red opened the bag and carefully emptied its contents onto the stone floor. Inside were a couple of magazines, a digital camera, a half-full water bottle, Altoids and three four-once glass jars carefully wrapped in bubble wrap, the tops secured with sealing tape. The jars contained a thick honey-colored liquid, and each was labeled with a string of numbers.

"What's this?" Red demanded to know, holding one of the jars.

"None of your business!" Lucia responded, her voice quivering. "It's just something I came up with. It's for bee stings. It's nothing. It's mine. *Give it to me!*"

"Quiet!" Red snarled. He stared first at the girl and then at the jars. He considered opening the jar and was about to when caution got the better of him. What if it was some sort of lethal chemical, he thought. She's just a bitty girl. Better to let someone else worry about it. Besides, he had it now, and he'd done what he'd been paid to do.

He rewrapped the jars and put them and the rest of the items back into the bag. He set the bag down near Lucia and Nikita to keep an eye on the girls and the prize.

"Whatever it is, it's ours now," he said.

CHAPTER THIRTY-EIGHT

April 25, 2:46 A.M., Lights End, Lylian

"ARANCK, IT IS GOOD TO SEE YOU, my friend," Laszlo said. "It seems you get another chance to perform on festival day."

"I have two squads, including Rowtag and Chepi," Aranck said.

Laszlo looked at the tiny warriors and nodded. "You, Rowtag and Chepi alone would be plenty. I estimate there are perhaps two dozen intruders and a few Lylian accomplices. I have four Rangers outside, and they've already disabled four of their guards.

"But we need to be careful. They took the serum," Laszlo said.

"We know," Rowtag said. That is why we are here."

"We need to break them up into smaller groups," Laszlo said to the Lytles huddled around him. "We need to confuse them. *Zurzavar Hoz Ellenség!*"

They talked for several minutes and agreed on a plan of action. Immediately Laszlo contacted Charles. "I think I found our diversion," he said.

"What is it?" Charles asked.

"Reinforcements," Laszlo whispered into his mic. "We have Lytles."

"We questioned one of the guards," Katie said into her mike. "There are a total of 30 men. They also brought along coyotes trained to kill. The animals are tethered on a lower level."

"We'll watch for them," Lazlo said. "Look for the signal, and *Zurzavar Hoz Ellenség!*"

Seven Meks rode quietly up the stairs to the first sublevel and dismounted their cats. The cats scurried down the hall to wait. The room holding Nikita and Lucia had two doors at opposite ends. The Lytles walked silently down the hall, keeping to the shadows. When the hallway reached the intersection, three Lytles went left and four went right to reach the two entrances.

About 20 feet from each door hung two battery-powered lanterns shedding light into the holding room. Rowtag and Chepi, one at each door, pulled a small metal ball from leather pouches on their belts and fit them into the end of their flick swords. Giving each other a signal, they each took aim at the lantern nearest them. Lifting swords high overhead, with a practiced flick they opened them to full length in a whip-like motion, toward the lights. The tiny ball bearings flew forward like bullets, breaking the lights and casting the room into pitch-black darkness.

A moment after the lights went out, gunshots were heard from the sublevels and from outside.

"We're under attack," Red screamed. He turned on his flashlight and used it like a pointer. "Get those lights back on. You four go up and reconnoiter—find out what they're shooting at. You four go see what's going on below. *Now!* Move it!"

Flashlights waved frantically all over the room as eight of the remaining 23 men followed the commands. Two of the men worked on the hallway lanterns to swap out the broken bulbs with new ones. Once finished, the men turned them back on, illuminating the room.

For a moment the Lytles were not even noticed.

Then one of the mercenaries looked toward the girls sitting on the floor and gasped.

"My God. It is true. They exist!" he shouted.

The seven Lytles stood next to the girls.

"What the …?" Red said.

The men forgot the excitement of the past few minutes and simply gaped at the tiny intruders. In the course of their training they had been instructed that on Lylian there were more than just humans to worry about. They were told about the dangerous little people who also inhabited the island, but most simply didn't believe it. The thought that some 10-inch freakazoid was any match for a soldier only made them laugh.

Lucia lay huddled, clutching her knees with her arms to protect her bruised ribs. Nikita knelt beside her. The seven Meks formed into a loose circle around the girls, arms at their sides, their attention focused on the mercenaries surrounding them.

The men pointed at them and laughed even more as the Lytles stood to protect the girls. The seven Meks remained still, watching the humans towering around them.

Finally Red spoke to his troops, their Uzi submachine guns on the floor at their feet. "Enough, dispose of them!" Red said, and the men reached for their weapons.

"Shoot them," Red commanded.

Before the soldiers could act the seven Meks threw their right arms across their bodies, grabbed their flick swords and, in unison, unsheathed the swords. They extended them 16 lengths and brought seven of the intruders down, each with a single plunge to the heart.

The mercenaries fell dead and bedlam began.

CHAPTER THIRTY-NINE

April 25, 3:12 A.M., Lights End, Lylian

UNAWARE OF THE FIGHTING TAKING PLACE INSIDE, four mercenaries peered cautiously out of the mammoth tower entrance. Using hand signals to communicate, they adjusted their night-vision goggles and quietly filtered out the door.

The grounds surrounding the tower were cluttered with huge chunks of stone that had fallen from the ancient structure over the years. The mercenaries separated, slowly picking their way through the debris looking for their comrades.

One soldier moving toward the truck guardedly stepped around the debris and noticed a bound body lying partially under the vehicle, apparently unconscious. Thinking it was one of his comrades, he walked over for a closer look.

"Günter, is that you?" he whispered.

"Sorry, the name's Hannah," she said, clobbering the soldier with a piece of stone and knocking him out. She removed the rope and jacket disguise she had taken from one of the guards and ducked into the shadows.

Emmett crawled, unseen, on top of an enormous slab of rock, silently watching a guard walk unknowingly toward him. When the guard passed directly beneath him, Emmett dropped down, landing a hard blow to the man.

Katie watched Emmett through her goggles as he tied up the guard. Distracted, she didn't hear the soldier sneak up behind her. She felt a gun barrel in her ribs.

"Well, looks like I caught me a girl … *and a pretty one at that,*" the soldier hissed in her ear.

Katie replied. "You're not afraid of a girl, are you?"

"Not a little one like you," he said, his gun moving slightly away from her body.

The moment his gun wavered, Katie leapt away and executed a quick scissors kick onto his chin, bringing him down with a thud.

"Well you should be," Katie said as she tied up the unconscious man.

Charles followed his target to the cliff's edge. He was within striking distance when the stones beneath his foot crunched, giving him away. The soldier swung around, but Charles was too fast and was on him before he could fire. The two struggled, fists and kicks pounding away relentlessly. Charles fell onto his back catching the soldier in the stomach with his legs. With a deep thrust, he flung him over the edge of the cliff, the guard screaming as he fell to the distant rocks below.

The guards neutralized, the four Rangers regrouped and discreetly entered the tower.

With the fighting happening outside and in the main room, four soldiers—following orders from Red—took off down the stairs. Motioning them by hand, they swept down the hallway. They first came to Laszlo's holding cell and discovered the dead soldier. They continued down the hallway to where it ended at another corridor that ran left and right. Two went left, the others right.

The two mercenaries moved slowly down the hall. Suddenly

from the shadows, 12 cats pounced, clawing and biting at them. The attack was so sudden and vicious the men could not reach their guns and could only try to protect themselves from being clawed and bitten to death.

"Arrgh, get off me!" one man yelled.

Two other soldiers walking the opposite direction ran back toward the commotion. As they raced ahead, a very thin rope was pulled tight across their path at ankle height and they came crashing to the floor with a thud, their guns clattering across the stone floor. With swords drawn to knife length, seven Lytles quickly surrounded the men. The men knew they were captured and did nothing but glare at their captors. The Lytles bound them with cord no thicker than thread but stronger than rope, then hurried to help the cats.

The two mercenaries continued to battle the cats. Flinging a Persian down the hall, one of them managed to break free. *"Bite me, will you?"* He leapt to his feet and ran off into the shadows of the hallway in search of stairs. Several cats went after him, but without the element of surprise, they could not tackle him again.

Laszlo dove on the man still covered in cats. He grabbed the man's hands and tied them behind his back. Once secured, the cats left him alone and began cleaning their paws, feeling very satisfied.

"Where's the fourth man?" Laszlo asked. Nosh indicated which direction he ran. "Go find the others; I'll take care of him."

As Laszlo ran down the hall in pursuit, Emmett reported in. "Laszlo, we've taken down four more. What's going on inside?"

"We've disabled three down here. I don't know what's going on above us. Rowtag and others went to free the girls. I'm after one who got away. I think he's trying to free the coyotes. Go help Rowtag. I'll stop the coyotes," Laszlo said.

———

Lucia was stunned by the sudden attack. She had never anticipated the little creatures could be so fierce, and she watched in horror as the mercenaries gathered their senses and prepared to counter-attack. But the Meks did not hesitate. They expanded their circle in a fluid motion, cutting at the ankles of the closest humans. The mercenaries fell with a wail, immobilized.

"Follow me," Rowtag told the girls as he moved toward's safety.

"Not without this," Lucia said. She grabbed her backpack and quickly followed Rowtag out of the room.

The remaining Lytles hid behind the fallen bodies. The mercenaries were not able to get clear shots and the Lytles continued to pick away at them with their flick swords until the mercenaries were down to just four men.

Hannah, Charles, Emmett and Katie appeared with Tasers aimed. The battle was over, and Gunnery Sergeant Red White was feeling very black and blue.

"Where are they taking us?" Lucia asked.

The Lytles led the girls quickly to a stairway going down into darkness. Chepi was in the lead, and Rowtag watched the rear, both with their swords out at medium length. Lucia clung to her backpack.

Nikita spoke to the Lytles in their language.

"They are taking us to a safe place," Nikita said. "They want us to hurry."

They went down the steep stairs two levels and met up with the other Lytles, who had just captured the three mercenaries. The Lytles and Nikita spoke quickly, bringing each other up to date.

"We must go down further, Lucia," Nikita said. "Don't worry, we will be safe. Laszlo is below."

They started down another stairway, and as they approached the fourth level, they could hear the barking rage of the coyotes growing closer.

Laszlo cursed himself for letting the mercenary get away. He flew down the stairs, his flick sword in hand. The intense noise of the coyotes' growling and barking did not deter him. He was on the fourth level, a floor comprising crisscrossing hallways and many small rooms. Working his way toward the howling and dim light of a room, he crept silently in case the mercenary was hiding and ready to jump him.

Laszlo leaned in from the corner and looked around. The mercenary had just arrived but had not yet untied the coyotes. Without warning, a huge fist slammed into the side of his face and Laszlo went down, the mercenary kicking him in the side as the coyotes went wild only a few feet from the fight.

Despite the hard fall, Laszlo still held tight to his flick sword. The mercenary bent down and lifted Laszlo up, taking his arm and smashing the sword against the stone wall with a force that snapped it at the fifth knuckle and destroyed the locking mechanism. The sword now hung limply at Laszlo's side. The mercenary looked at the broken sword with satisfaction and reached for a gun lying near the coyotes. He pointed it at Laszlo.

"You've ruined my sword!" Laszlo said in amazement, oblivious to the danger facing him.

"That's not all I'm ruining. I don't know who you are, but I know what you are—dead," the mercenary spat.

Though the remaining metal in Laszlo's hand might have been rendered worthless as a sword, it was far from useless. Laszlo whipped the broken weapon at the man's neck, the metal coiling tightly and strangling him. As the mercenary fell to the ground, his gun skidded across the floor, into the pack of coyotes and out of Laszlo's reach.

The coyotes now were frenzied, salivating as they pulled at the ropes holding them. One or two started biting at the thin ropes to free themselves, and soon the entire pack was chewing through their bonds. Without a way to get to the gun or contain the straining animals, Laszlo ran from the doorless room to warn the others.

He raced through the labyrinth of corridors toward the stairwell and arrived just as the Lytles came down with Lucia and Nikita.

"We haven't much time." Laszlo said. "They brought coyotes with them. They're tied but chewing through their ropes. We need to get out of here."

"I hear them!" Lucia cried.

Immediately the barking grew close. Without warning, a coyote sprang from the darkness right at Laszlo. He grabbed the animal by the neck, falling backwards, and threw it into the darkness behind him. It scurried away to wait for the pack. Laszlo could see its yellow eyes watching from the shadows.

Down the stairs came Emmett, Katie, Charles and Hannah. "We've secured the upper floors," Charles said. "I think we got them all."

"There's a pack of crazed coyotes running free down here. Let's head up!" Laszlo yelled.

The remaining Lytles joined them, and all started back up the stairs when machine-gun fire began raining down on them. The group quickly got off the steps and away from the shooting.

"I thought you said you got them," Laszlo shouted.

"We did, every intruder is accounted for," Emmett insisted.

From above, voices shouted down.

"Zurzavar Hoz Ellenség! You forgot about us, eh?" Sascha shouted. "You'll not come up this way. And soon those animals will eat you

for dinner."

"Lylians!" Laszlo said. "It was easy for them to hide. They know this place as well as us. Blast it. Quick, look for anything to hold off the coyotes. The Tasers are already spent."

The Black Army Rangers looked around for loose stones or sticks, anything. The group spoke quickly in the strange language Lucia did not understand.

From the shadows they could hear the coyotes closing in, biding their time before attacking. They were cunning and had spread out to attack from all corridors.

"Lucia, Nikita, you must go with the Lytles," Laszlo said. "Protect the serum. We will block the way. Go."

The hallways erupted with charging coyotes. Half the Lytles took off down the stairwell with Lucia carrying her backpack, while the other half, riding their cats, charged the coyotes. The Rangers began throwing rocks and using the sticks like bludgeons. The coyotes were relentless. The Rangers held off the beasts as best they could, but half a dozen coyotes managed to get by and ran down the steps toward the fleeing group.

Headlong they ran, Lucia's bruised side throbbing in pain. Nikita was just a step or two ahead of her. They went down three more levels and were almost to the large copper door and the safety of the cable car room. Chepi jumped from her cat and opened the copper door with her flick sword.

The coyotes burst into the large room snarling and barking. The Lytles spun around to fight them off and form a circle barrier around Lucia and Nikita. The coyotes growled and raged in frustration at the tiny warriors.

The seven slowly edged their way back toward the door and pushed Nikita and Lucia into the cable room.

The coyotes, sensing their prey was going to escape, pounced, teeth bared. The Lytles took down the first two with their flick swords. The remaining four animals became more cautious, but no less dangerous. Four more coyotes that managed to get past the defenders upstairs soon joined them. This emboldened the pack and they moved closer.

With Lucia, Nikita and most of the Lytles safely below, the six Lytles whistled and up ran their cats from the cable car room. The coyotes went wild with excitement. The Lytles leapt to their saddles and charged the coyotes. The coyotes rushed forward as a pack. Just before they clashed, the cats jumped clear over them, landing behind the line of animals. The coyotes pivoted to face their prey, but the cats held their ground as the Lytles drove their swords into the animals, killing them.

The Lytles stayed on their cats, viewing the carnage, satisfied the animals could do no more harm. Now, however, with their backs turned to the stairwell, up and out of the darkness a lone coyote jumped silently at the group. It grabbed Aranck in its jaws, tearing him off Bátor and crushing his body in its canine vice. The coyote flung the limp Aranck across the chamber and turned to make another attack. Meeting it halfway were the piercing blades of five flick swords, as Chepi and Rowtag cried out in rage.

Aranck lay motionless on the cold stone floor. Bátor sat by his side gently licking his face. The Lytles picked up their comrade and carried him down to the cable car room.

Moments later Laszlo and the four other Rangers joined the rest there and closed the door.

"Lucia, Nikita, are you all right?" Laszlo asked.

"We're fine," the girls weakly answered as one.

As Laszlo went to comfort the two girls, Chepi, Nosh and the other Lytles drew their swords and surrounded the Rangers.

"What's the meaning of this?" Laszlo asked. "We're your friends. We're not the enemy."

The Lytles said nothing but held them at bay.

"Come with me," Alawa said. She motioned Lucia toward the open cargo car.

"What do you want me to do?" she asked with growing alarm.

"I think they want you to get in," Nikita said, helpless to interfere.

Alawa gently but firmly pushed Lucia into the open car. She got in and sat down with her knees folded underneath and her arms at her side like a small sphinx. The Lytles quickly tossed ropes over her and tied her firmly into the car so she could not be tossed out. They added a car behind her, carefully placed her backpack inside and tied it firmly into place as well.

Finally they placed Aranck into one of the closed carriages. Those not guarding the Rangers joined him.

"Nikita, where are they taking me?" Lucia cried out. Dazed and confused by all that had happened, Lucia had thought she was finally safe. Now she was being kidnapped again, only this time it was the Lytles who had her.

"Lucia, be strong," Laszlo assured her. "I don't know what is happening, but I know you will be safe."

Wordlessly, Chepi and Nosh guarded the Rangers, never looking away, as the cable cars slowly moved out of the station and into the black tunnel.

Chapter Forty

April 25, 4:31 A.M., Lights End, Lylian

LUCIA WAS TERRIFIED. She craned her head to look behind her and saw the light of the room gradually disappear as the cable car slowly moved away. She had no idea what was happening. She thought she had been saved, and now she was on some weird amusement park ride that wasn't at all amusing.

After her eyes finally adjusted, she could take in the tunnel, which had been carefully and smoothly cut from the mountain rock and lit by other, stranger rocks that glowed dimly.

The cable car started to pick up speed. Soon they were racing along. The wind whipped through her hair as the train sped up and down through the carved earth. Every so often, the train emerged into larger open caves, and high overhead, she could see incredible stalactites hanging. Then, just as quickly, the train would re-enter the tunnel; Lucia was certain if she lifted her head an inch it would get knocked off.

The ride went on for miles and miles, at times slowing down to a crawl as the cable car made a particularly high climb, only to plunge down the other side at breakneck speed. After what seemed like an eternity, the train finally came out of the tunnel, but this time into cool open air. Lucia breathed deeply from it and tried to get her bearings. The sun was just beginning to appear ahead of her in the eastern sky as the cable car picked up speed again and raced up and over the mountains. She had no idea where she was. The landscape was strange to her. The cable car passed through a few more tunnels and then slowed as they came to the shores of a lake and finally stopped.

It was now early morning, and the sun peeked through the trees that surrounded the lake. The station was a simple open wooden platform, and Lucia sat there, helpless, still tied to the cable car.

The Lytles stepped out of the cable car. Lucia thought they would release her, but first they untied her backpack and carefully checked the contents. Then several of them carried it away. Once the bag was safely removed, they came over to her.

The Lytles quietly stood and looked at Lucia. They did not say a word but slowly smiled at her. Finally one of them spoke.

"Do not be afraid, Lucia. I am Rowtag. You are safe here."

Rowtag gently untied her, and Lucia shakily got to her feet and stumbled from the car. Her knees ached from being folded under her for so long, her shins were bruised from the ride, her ribs throbbed, and she was covered in dried spaghetti sauce. Other than that, she felt fine.

"Where am I?" she asked.

"We have taken you to safety," Rowtag replied. "We have brought you to The Tilt."

"*The Tilt!*" Lucia exclaimed and looked around her.

At first glance it looked just like any woods next to a lake, but, on closer examination, she found many of the trees embedded with doors or abutted by tiny buildings. In a moment she realized these were not just a few dwellings but an entire town that sprawled far and wide.

It was now dawn and the town was coming awake. The Lytle

climbed a miniature tower and started ringing a bell to announce their arrival. Soon doors started opening and sleepy Lytles began filing out to see what the commotion was all about. They stared up in disbelief at an actual human being standing in The Tilt for the first time any of them could remember. Lytle children, no taller than a person's thumb, clung to their parents at the wonder of seeing a human for the first time. Soon Lucia was surrounded by hundreds of Lytles.

Rowtag told the gathering crowd of the battle of Light's End. The little people stood silent as they listened to the tale of the failed mercenaries and their vicious coyotes. He used his flick sword to illustrate a particular fight scene, and the crowd cheered with pride.

Finally Rowtag spoke very solemnly and then motioned to Alawa, who brought out Lucia's backpack. They opened it, reached inside and pulled out the honey-colored jars. Alawa said something to the crowd in their shared tongue while she raised the serum for all to see. The Lytles erupted in cheers and shouts of joy. Lucia looked across their faces and saw mothers and fathers weeping and holding their children close to them. Others started dancing and hugging. Then a low chant arose from the crowd in words Lucia could not begin to understand.

Rowtag spoke again to the crowd, causing them to quiet. He turned to Lucia and bowed.

"They would like to hear from you, Lucia," he said. "You are their hero."

"Me? A hero?" she said. "All I did was get captured."

"You did much more than that, Lucia," Rowtag said. "You have saved our lives. I will tell you more later, but first they would like to hear from you."

Lucia looked around at the throng of Lytles gazing up at her, their green sashes the color of the forest around them. It dawned on her who they were. "Um, hello, are you all Meks?" she asked the crowd.

And they went wild with more chanting: *"Meks ... Meks ... Meks ... Meks ... ,"* delighted that she knew their tribe.

"Um, thank you for saving me and bringing me here. It is an honor, and well, it's just great to see you all."

Rowtag translated and they cheered again and danced around her.

Alawa said, "Now leave our new friend to rest. She has been through a great deal."

The Lytles gave a final cheer and went back to their homes, leaving as quickly as they appeared.

"Come with me, Lucia, we have much to talk about," Rowtag said. He led her to a small clearing behind them.

They sat silently together before Rowtag spoke.

"I believe by now you've heard the story of how the humans came to this island many, many years ago. When they first arrived there were many Lytles who wanted to kill them all. They thought the humans would bring nothing but trouble. Others remembered that, before the Great Catastrophe, humans and Lytles had lived together in harmony on the island. It was decided to let them live. For over 400 years we have lived in guarded harmony. While there have been some Lytles who would like to see the humans gone, there sadly have been more humans who wished we were gone."

Lucia sat spellbound listening to the Lytle, barely 10 inches tall, tell her this story.

"Almost 50 years ago, there was an evil human leader on the island. This Navigator, as they call their leaders, wanted all the Lytles killed. There was no way he could attack us directly, so he did it in another, far more clever way. He created a disease. A disease that affected only Lytles—and would eventually kill us all."

"A disease?" Lucia asked.

"Yes, and now almost all Lytles have contracted it. It was incurable. Until now."

"A cure? That's great news. But where did the cure come from?"

"It came from you!"

Lucia thought of the jars of honey-colored liquid she had been so protective of. "Ohmygosh, you mean the stuff in my jars is the medicine?"

"Yes, it is."

"I was just trying to develop something so bee stings wouldn't hurt. I wrote about it in my blog and even got it reviewed in a medical magazine," Lucia said. "I've been wondering this whole time why you wanted it."

"That is how your serum was discovered," Rowtag said. "For many years doctors and scientists on the island have searched for a cure. One of them came across the article about your discovery, and it caught his eye. While it might also sooth bee stings, we hoped it could be the treatment we were desperate for. That was just a few months ago. When we contacted your father, he sent us a sample, and with a little modification, it worked."

"Why all the secrecy?" Lucia asked. "Why not just have us send it over? I would have given it to you for nothing."

"Because if word had gotten out, the *A Törvényes*, The Rightful, would have stopped at nothing to destroy the serum. That would have included killing your entire family. We believed The Rightful were plotting to take over the island, but until last night we did not know when or how.

"Once we saw the danger you were in at Light's End, we knew

we had to bring you and the serum back here immediately, for your safety and for the future of the Lytles."

"What's happening now?" Lucia asked. "Is the fighting over?"

"We are waiting for messengers to return from Corvinus with news. We believe it is over, but until we are certain, you will remain here."

"How is Aranck?" Lucia asked. "Is, is he all right? He was so fearless."

"We don't know," Rowtag replied. "He was severely hurt. He is being cared for right now. Come, you must be exhausted. Rest here while we wait for word. I will have food and drink brought to you."

With that, Rowtag, Alawa and the others left her under the shade of the trees on the soft grass. Lucia sat and thought about the life-changing events of the last few days and how very far away she felt from home. Her eyes were closed when something nudged her shoulder, and she opened them to see Bátor nuzzling against her.

"Oh, you were so brave back there!" she said as she scratched his head. Bátor still wore his saddle, and Lucia removed it and scratched his back as he purred contentedly. "I'm so sorry about Aranck," she said. Lucia continued stroking the cat until she sank into a deep, dreamless sleep.

Chapter Forty-One

April 25, 5:00 A.M., Lights End, Lylian

"Where are they taking her?" Nikita asked. "Will she be all right?"

"I'm certain she will be fine." Laszlo said. "My guess is they took her to The Tilt. They have their serum now. That is all they care about. Come, we've waited long enough, let's gather up the prisoners and get out of here."

They walked up and out of the lower levels. By the time they reached the entrance, a platoon of Rangers stood guard with guns drawn. In the center was the tall figure of General Rutger.

The General called out. "Laszlo, over here. Where's the girl?"

Laszlo quickly filled in the General on the battle and the Lytles' escape with Lucia and the serum.

"They took the girl back to The Tilt?" the General exclaimed. *"The Tilt?"*

"That's my guess, sir," Laszlo answered. "I had no idea there was a cable car route to this side of the island. The level is very hidden. It must be centuries old."

The General paused, deep in thought. Finally he spoke.

"There's nothing more we can do here. Take the prisoners back to town and throw them in the brig. We'll deal with them later. Mr. Boyd is with your father at the house. I suggest we go there and wait for the Lytles to contact us."

The army vehicles raced quickly back to Corvinus and over the bridges to Matthias Island. The sun was bright in the morning sky as General Rutger, Laszlo and Nikita entered the house and found Jakob Corvinus and Leo sitting outside on the veranda, drinking coffee.

Upon seeing the group cross the garden, Leo jumped to his feet and hurried toward them. "Lucia, where's Lucia? Is she all right?"

"We believe she is safe, Mr. Boyd," General Rutger said as calmly as he could.

Laszlo took over to explain the events following their kidnapping from the festival.

"Why did the Lytles take her?" Leo demanded.

"I believe they felt only they could keep the serum safe," the General said. "Otherwise, if it is true they took her to The Tilt, that would be highly unusual."

"Can you call them?" Leo wanted to know. "Do they even have phones?"

"They have an emissary's office north of town," Jakob said. "We have somebody waiting there now. When the Lytles make contact, we will know. Come Leo, try and remain calm. She will be treated well; they will not hurt her. The serum is safely where it should be."

"My God, I had no idea what I was getting into!" Leo exclaimed. "I thought there might be some excitement, but had I known, I would never have brought my daughter into such a dangerous situation."

"Rest assured, Mr. Boyd, the worst is over," the General said. "We had the opportunity to question several of the prisoners, including their leader, a fellow named Red. Apparently they were the spearhead for a takeover of our island. They were to secure the airport for the arrival of two 747s carrying more than a thousand mercenaries."

"Where are the planes now?" Leo asked. "Will they land?"

"No, they never received orders to do so," the General said. "They've been in the air circling for hours waiting for the signal. They are still somewhere overhead not far from here. Even now our Captain is phoning the U.S. president to tell him of the coup attempt. He will order the United States to scramble some fighter jets to bring them down on American soil and arrest them for crimes against humanity."

"The president will do that for you?" Leo asked incredulously.

"Yes, he will be happy to do so. We have information to trade on a certain Middle Eastern nation they are very interested in learning more about. They will be more than eager to help us."

A moment later an aid to the General came up to him and whispered in his ear.

"Excellent, thank you," the General said. "Mr. Boyd. Good news, your daughter is indeed safe and in The Tilt. We've just heard from the Lytles and they are going to bring her to the border. Come, we'll take my car."

Chapter Forty-Two

April 25, 8:47 A.M., The Tilt, Lylian

Lucia woke up with Bátor still sleeping on her stomach. She looked around and found herself surrounded by tiny Lytles, both adults and children. She rubbed her eyes to make certain she wasn't dreaming.

"Have I been asleep long?" she asked. She looked at the sky to see the sun very high and bright.

Next to her was a bowl filled with water for her to drink. As she drank, she had the notion it might be someone's bathtub.

"Thank you. I was very thirsty," she said.

Shyly, several young Lytle children awkwardly approached her, carrying an enormous bouquet of cut wildflowers as tall as themselves. They dropped it beside her and scurried back to the others.

"Oh, you are so kind!" she said. She scooped up the flowers and pressed them to her face.

The crowd clapped and started singing in their language.

They had been entertaining Lucia for some time when Rowtag interrupted the performance. "It is time to go. Your friends are eager to have you back."

"Ohmygosh, my dad's going to be mad!" she said.

"No, Lucia, I think he is going to be very happy," Rowtag said. "Come with me. You will enjoy one more ride on our cable cars. A shorter one."

Lucia scratched Bátor once more behind the ears and set him down on the grass beside her. "I'm going to miss you, fella."

"Before we go, someone wants to thank you personally," Rowtag said.

Who could that be? Lucia wondered as they walked toward a Lytle-sized hospital constructed around the base of a green ash tree. Naturally it was far too small for Lucia to enter, so she waited outside as Rowtag went in.

A few minutes later several Meks carried out a small bed. There lay Aranck. He was very weak, but healing.

"You're alive!" Lucia said. "I am so happy you weren't killed by that vicious animal." She bent down to gently tuck the covers around him.

In a weak voice Aranck responded, "I was the first to say you could save us. I was there in Budapest secretly watching over you at your hotel and around the city. I have been protecting you for some time. Only, I did not do as well as I wanted. I am sorry they captured you. I am glad we were able to rescue you."

"You saved me," Lucia said. "It's simple as that. What's more, I believe in you. Now you must get well. I know Bátor misses you."

"Farewell, Lucia Boyd," the Lytle said. "We will sing ballads about today and your family for a very long time."

With those words his friends carried him back inside. Lucia followed Rowtag down to the lake and to a cable car station along the shore.

"I am afraid for your safety; I must secure you in the car with these ropes, Lucia," he said.

"That's all right—I'm ready for it this time," she reassured him.

"You may enjoy this ride more, as it is mostly in the open air," he said. "We will take you to the Kemeks' tribal village and transfer there to another cable car that will take us to the border of The Tilt, and to your father."

The Meks tied Lucia into one cargo car, and her backpack, minus the serum, into another.

"Are you ready?" Rowtag asked.

"As ready as I'll ever be," she answered.

With Alawa as conductor, the cable car picked up speed immediately and bolted out of the station *"Woohee!"* Lucia shouted as the car flew down a steep hillside. Across The Tilt, it raced up and down hilltops and whisked over wide-open glens. It was the rollercoaster ride of a lifetime. "I'd even pay money for this," she thought as the car banked into a sharp turn and ducked into a tunnel and out again.

At the Kemek village the car slowed to a stop. The Meks were intent on getting Lucia back to her family quickly, but the Kemeks insisted that she say a few words. Rowtag got out and untied Lucia, who rose gingerly and stretched her legs. She looked around and there were thousands of Kemeks greeting her. They were slightly larger than the Meks and wore bright red sashes across their chests.

Lucia took in the virtual sea of Kemek Lytles surrounding her, recognizing them by their sashes. "Hello," she said. "Thank you for stopping by to welcome me. I am very happy to meet so many brave Kemeks."

When she said their tribal name, they roared with approval and threw their hats high into the air. One of the Kemeks came up to her and removed his red sash and handed it to her with a bow.

And then the Kemek tour ended, almost before it had begun. The entire village sang goodbye to Lucia as her Mek escorts scooted her into the next cable car for the final ride back to her father.

This time the cable car took off more slowly but took on a

mountainside that seemed to go straight up. "What's coming next?" she said to herself. A moment later she found out. The cable car had reached the crest of the mountain then shot straight down into a valley and right back up another one. Lucia thought she might throw up but at the same time hoped the ride would never end. The trip continued on that way for another few nerve-wracking minutes, when finally it came to the edge of a fast-moving river and made one final duck through a tunnel under the river and up to the other side.

The cable car rolled to a stop in a thicket of bushes, and Rowtag and the Meks released Lucia so she could stand and stretch her legs. Ahead of her she could see her father standing with General Rutger, Laszlo, Nikita and Jakob, along with a dozen or so very serious-looking border soldiers.

Lucia stepped out of the bushes and waved to the group. "Dad! Over here! I'm fine." She ran to her father.

"Lucia! Thank God you're safe. I was so worried." Leo picked her up in a hug and swung her off the ground and around.

The Lytles emerged a moment later, their hands resting gently on their swords. The General saw them and bowed deeply from the waist.

"Thank you, Meks," he said. "Rowtag, you have done well. We are, once again, in your debt."

Lucia looked at the tiny Lytles, so proud and fearless, standing before her. She bent down to speak to them. "I cannot thank you enough for what you did for me. I will always cherish my visit to The Tilt. You have been so kind to me."

Lucia reached up and removed her silver necklace with the small heart and handed it Rowtag. "This is my favorite necklace, and I want you to have it."

The Mek looked at it for a moment and then lifted it high and cried out, *"Zurzavar Hoz Ellenség!"*

CHAPTER FORTY-THREE

April 25, 9:54 A.M., Under the Atlantic Ocean

THE MEN SAT TOGETHER IN THE KITCHEN GALLEY, proud of their submarine, the crew and their captain who had brought them safely out of the harrowing seas.

"Captain, we have a story to pass down like no other," one of the crew said, and toasted the captain with his vodka glass.

"*Salut!*" they all concurred.

They were safely underway, 400 feet under the cold Atlantic Ocean. The men were celebrating their victory with an immense sense of relief. Many had thought they would be sailing into a watery grave.

But the mission was over. They had succeeded.

Vladimir was proud of his men. They had been brave and true. They had sailed into the very jaws of death and out again. And now it seemed like it happened so long ago, when in fact only a day had passed since they broke surface off Lylian.

Vladimir knew they were doubly lucky to be alive. He swirled the vodka in his glass with one hand while the other held the detonator to a bomb he had discovered and disarmed. The Count had hidden an explosive device on the submarine timed to go off eight hours after the landing commenced. Apparently he didn't want to take any chances answering to the World Court about how he'd gained

control of Lylian. He was not about to give the United Nations—
nor any world power—the slightest chance of intervening in Lylian.
Fortunately, one of the coyotes had used that storage locker as a toilet,
and when the crew cleaned up the mess, they discovered the device.

"I never thought I would say these words, but, 'Thank God for
those coyotes,' " Vladimir said, and the men toasted once again.

Vladimir knew there was no use going back to Mauritania. The
boat was never meant to return, and by now the submarine base was
probably scuttled. They would travel farther down the coast of Africa
to Liberia. There was a large and active arms and military supply
market there, and he knew this Victor II class submarine would fetch
a very handsome sum.

He would divide the money equally with the crew. That would
more than double what the Count had promised them and ensure a
happy, uneventful journey home for all.

CHAPTER FORTY-FOUR

April 25, 10:34 P.M., Corvinus, Lylian

THE FIRST STOP AFTER RETURNING TO CORVINUS was the hospital for a thorough exam for Lucia. Jakob insisted, as did Laszlo and Nikita, that the Boyds spend their remaining days on Lylian, at their home on Matthias Island. While Lucia was being examined at the hospital, Leo and Nikita went to the hotel to pack up their things.

Sonja and Sven had been extremely concerned for Lucia and had already heard some of the news from Light's End. It was, after all, a very small island, and with 20 Rangers protecting Leo and Navigator Jakob Corvinus, they knew something very big had happened.

The troop returned to the hospital to find that Lucia was deemed in good enough shape to leave. They drove off to the Corvinus estate for rest and recuperation.

Once they arrived, Lucia and Nikita excused themselves to clean up and rest.

"Father, if you'll excuse me, it was a long night for me as well. I'll give you a complete report in a few hours," Laszlo said.

"Get some rest, son. You did well. Very well." Jakob embraced his son.

Laszlo left the room, leaving Jakob and Leo alone together.

"Leo, I assume this was more than you had in mind for your journey here. I am sorry we put you in so much danger. We simply didn't know the extent of the situation."

"I still don't understand how Lucia's bee sting remedy could be so valuable to you," Leo said.

"Let's have breakfast on the veranda, and I will explain," Jakob said.

Jakob waited until a butler brought them coffee and took their requests for breakfast. By now it was almost noon, and although neither had slept the previous night, they were both wide awake on adrenalin.

As Jakob explained the whole story, Leo stared at his eggs in disbelief.

"We did our best to protect you while you were here and at the same time be discreet. Whenever we could, your daughter had the protection of one of our best Black Army Rangers—my son, Laszlo."

Leo reached into his pocket, pulled out a tiny leather pouch and handed it to Jakob. "This was given to Lucia by Aranck on our first night on the island, when he gave her the blue flower. What you've told me explains the note inside."

Jakob frowned and opened the pouch to remove the tiny note inside. On the silver blue piece of paper were the words, "We believe in you."

"I had no idea what it meant. Now I do."

The butler came and cleared the breakfast dishes as the two men sat in silence watching island birds fly in and around the gardens.

"What will become of the mercenaries?" Leo asked.

"They will be returned to whatever country they call home. And they will be paid to keep their silence about what they've seen. Our fight is not with them. But if they do not cooperate, we have threatened to turn them over to the Lytles, and of that they are terrified. Now, rest! We will have visitors for dinner. Friends of your daughter will be stopping by."

The Boyds, Nikita and Laszlo slept most of the day and finally woke in the late afternoon. One by one they came down and sat in the garden, in the dimming rays of warm sunshine.

When Laszlo finally joined them, Lucia jumped from her chair and ran to give him a hug. "Laszlo, you are my hero. You saved us all!"

"I made them a special!" Laszlo laughed. "Hannah, Emmett, Katie and Charlie played a big part as well, to say nothing of the real heroes, the Lytles."

Laszlo explained how he was led away to the lower-level cell but had the good fortune to keep his smartphone—therefore access to his flick sword.

"Wait! So you haven't been listening to music this whole time?" Lucia asked in astonishment.

Nikita answered for him. "Well, certainly sometimes. He's very partial to *The Rolling Stones*. But you must understand, Lucia, the best way to hide is in the open. And who would ever have guessed that some music-listening rocker, seemingly oblivious to anything around him, is in fact a Ranger in the Black Army and your guardian?"

The group was still updating each other when the General arrived with Jakob.

"General Rutger, any more news?" Laszlo asked as he stood at loose attention.

"Sit down, son, relax. You've done your work. Between the captured soldiers and The Rightful Lylians, we have a pretty good idea who was involved. And the very good news is that I understand the Lytles have already started inoculating their population with the serum. All in all, a very good outcome for everyone."

As dusk came, staff started preparing the long outdoor table for dinner.

Lucia absently watched them set the table. She noticed they set places for eight on one side and none on the other. Then she got very excited as the servers placed a tiny table, no more than a ledge, on top of the table, including eight tiny chairs and matching dinnerware.

"Are Lytles coming to dinner?" she asked hopefully.

"Yes," Nikita replied, "along with Wan Foo Chan and MeLee. You see, they are the scientists who first discovered your serum online. They were the ones who truly realized its remarkable potential."

A few moments later, Wan Foo and MeLee joined the happy group.

Wan Foo immediately swept up Lucia to give her a big hug. "I've heard you were very brave!"

Lucia smiled and winced at the same time as Wan Foo hugged her bruised ribs. "Um, thanks. But I wasn't the bravest. That was Laszlo."

"Then I must hug Laszlo," Wan Foo said and hugged the hero.

The group talked and laughed and listened to each other's recounting of events. The sky had darkened, and the warm glow of light from the house and the twinkling outdoor lights made the whole evening magical. A waiter leaned in to quietly tell Jakob the other guests had arrived.

"Thank you," Jakob said. "Attention. Our guests of honor are here."

They all turned toward the French doors, and in came Rowtag, Alawa, Nosh and Chepi, each holding up the corner of a large wooden chest. Then came four more Lytles from the battle, also holding the corners of a large wooden box, only this one looked more like a small, ornate house. Then behind them came Bátor, who made his way to

Lucia and gently rubbed against her legs.

The servants replenished everyone's drinks in new glasses and offered the Lytles tiny goblets of *Kék Bor,* which they gladly accepted. The group sat down, the Lytles taking the smaller chairs on top of the table. Lucia looked at Rowtag, Alawa, Nosh and Chepi dressed in formal clothing with their dark green Mek sashes. She identified the other Lytles as two Kemeks in their bright red sashes and two Epps dressed in their fine woolen clothes spun from cat fur.

The group couldn't stop discussing the week's events, and even Rowtag joined in, delightfully recounting Lucia's cable car adventure through the Tilt countryside.

"I had no idea the Lytles had built a route all the way to Light's End," General Rutger said.

"That line is very old," Alawa replied. "There was a time when Light's End was the very center of activity on the island. But that was eons ago."

Dinner was ready, and they all sat down at the long table alight with candles. The dinner continued with laughter, toasts and requests for songs from everyone there. The Lytles sang in their own language, of times long ago. When dinner was over, the Lytles all solemnly stood and paused for a moment. Then without warning, they grabbed their flick swords and raised them as one. They released them to their full length and brought the tips together in a salute to the Boyds. Then they shouted out *"Zurzavar Hoz Ellenség! Confusion to the enemy!"* Their friends erupted in cheers. When the table had quieted again, the Lytles put away their swords but continued to stand.

"We have gifts for you," Rowtag said. "Leo Boyd, for your help in bringing your daughter to save us, there can be no reward large enough. But we would like you to accept this gift as a small way for us to say thank you."

214

One of the staff carried the hatbox-sized wooden case up to Leo and set it in front of him. Leo looked at the case for a moment and then opened it. Inside were stacks of gold coins and bags of diamonds, emeralds, rubies and other precious stones. It was a fortune many times more than Leo could have imagined. "I'm speechless! This is too much. Had I known of your plight we would have simply given you the serum."

"We are truly grateful," Nosh said.

Rowtag turned to Laszlo and spoke. "We understand your Flick Sword was destroyed in the battle."

"It's true," Laszlo confirmed. "It had been my constant companion since I was just a child. And it was you who taught me how to use it, even though you said no human could ever master it."

"You were determined to learn, and you were a good student. And now you're worthy of another flick sword." With that, Rowtag removed his own sword and handed it across the table to Laszlo.

Laszlo stood and bowed. "Thank you. I am truly honored." He released it to full length and just as quickly closed it again.

Lucia couldn't stop looking at all her new friends around the table. She wanted it to never be over. But it almost was, she knew. In a day or two, they would go home. Lost in her reverie, she almost didn't hear Rowtag addressing her.

"Lucia, we have not forgotten you. There is nothing adequate we could ever give you to show the depth of our thanks. Nevertheless, we have tried, and we have chosen something very special for you." Rowtag whistled once, and up on the table jumped Bátor.

"We would like to give you one of our most prized possessions, a Lytle cat, complete with his own traveling house. That is, if it is all right with your father."

"I think I'm outnumbered on this," Leo said.

"Lucia, you know his name is Bátor," Rowtag said. "But do you know what that means? In Lylian it means Brave One."

Bátor walked over to Lucia, and she picked him up as if she would never put him down. "Oh Dad, I know it's going to be all right. *Oh thank you, thank you, thank you!*"

The crowd at the table all clapped in approval. More songs were sung and the party went on until the moon was long gone.

Chapter Forty-Five

April 26, 3:43 A.M., Lake Neusiedler, Austria

THE COUNT WAS BESIDE HIMSELF. He had no idea what was happening on the ground in Lylian. It was now well over 24 hours since his last contact, and there had been no word. Now, to make matters worse, he had not been able to reach the transport jets for more than three hours.

He was very concerned for the success of his mission. The Count was worn with exhaustion, but too agitated to sleep. The sky was dimming in the early evening as he stared out the window across to the lake, when his phone rang. The number was known by only one person on Earth: Red White.

The Count dashed to the phone and answered immediately, his heart pounding. "Red! It's about time you called. Tell me of your success! Do you have the airport? Have the planes landed? What's happening?"

There was silence on the other end for what seemed like an eternity. Finally a small, deep voice spoke.

"Good evening, Count," the Mek said in Lylianese. "I hope I'm not interrupting anything important, but I thought you would like an update on your plan."

"Who is this?" the Count demanded. But deep down he knew. He recognized the accent and the fierce determination in the voice.

It was a Lytle—a Lytle in possession of his landing force's cellphone.

"Who I am is not as important as what I am," Rowtag replied. "But I believe you know what I am. Your plan has failed. The soldiers are all dead or captured, as are your pack of coyotes. And the second wave of invaders have been grounded and are by now in jail somewhere in the U.S., thanks to the assistance of the American government."

The Count glared across the room, his mind going a thousand directions at once. He had failed. All the planning, the time and money, all for nothing, and all destroyed by a race not a foot high.

Then he remembered his father's plague and smiled grimly. "You may have defeated my plan to take the island, but thanks to my father, you are all still doomed. Tell me Lytle, do you tell your children they are all dying?"

"There is no need to, Count. You see, the American girl whose invention you were so interested in became far more valuable to us than you could ever imagine. Her serum was nothing less than a cure for your father's evil infection."

"That's impossible," denied the Count.

"Nothing is impossible. We are cured. We are safe in the world once again, Count, unlike you. Goodbye. The next time we speak it will be in person."

The Count gasped for air and then stood very still, a tingle of dread running up his spine.

Rowtag didn't bother to hang up. He simply tossed the cellphone high into the air, grabbed his flick sword, and with one blur of motion cut it in two. He was thankful that General Rutger had let him be the one to call The Count and give him the news. He looked forward to his visit.

CHAPTER FORTY-SIX

April 29, 7:20 A.M., Matthias Island, Lylian

THE BOYDS SPENT THREE DAYS CONVALESCING (with a few souvenir shopping trips into town for Lucia). They also wanted to ensure that the Lytles could produce enough serum from Lucia's samples, and indeed they did. So all too soon the time came for them to leave Lylian.

Leo and Lucia got up early for their flight back to Minneapolis. The Captain of Lylian had arranged with America's president permission for the LylAir flight to go directly to Minneapolis rather than make a connection with Delta Airlines in Budapest.

Nikita, Laszlo, Jakob and the General escorted them to the airport. The air was cold in the early morning, and everyone was lost in thought.

"Lucia, it was such an adventure to have met you," Nikita said. "I will not forget this time we had together."

"Forget it? I could never ... ever ... forget anything about you, or your family, or Lylian or the Lytles or anything!"

"You must come back and visit us again," Jakob said. "Next time, bring your mother."

"She is going to die when I tell her what happened," Lucia said.

"I think you better leave that to me," Leo said. "No sense in having her arrest me for child endangerment."

There was much hugging, handshaking and backslapping as the two parties said goodbye. Bátor was safely tucked away in his elaborate traveling case and seemed very content. Once all were on board, the cabin was secured for departure and the plane taxied down the tarmac. The Boyds discovered they were the only passengers on the flight and were not surprised. After all, Minneapolis wasn't a scheduled stop from the island.

The galley door flew open and out came Singer, in full voice, to give the preflight instructions. She sang to the empty cabin as though it were a full house, and Leo and Lucia hummed along.

Their six-hour flight home was uneventful, and the time passed quickly.

"Dad," Lucia said, "I know it's been barely a week, but it seems like we left home a hundred years ago."

"I feel the same way," he agreed. "It will be good to see your mom again."

The plane landed in Minneapolis and the Boyds were hurried through customs without so much as a nod from the officials. It appeared that the Captain of Lylian's influence extended even here.

Outside of customs stood Lucia's mom, waving. "Peanut, welcome home!"

Lucia sprinted to her mother and gave her a huge hug. "Mom. You will never, *ever*, believe what we've done."

"Hello Martha, I missed you," Leo said. "We're home safe. And that's saying something."

"I see you brought home a new friend," Martha said, eyeing the cat in the cage.

"Oh, Mom, this cat literally saved my life. I have so much to tell you. But first I want to get home."

They loaded the car with their bags and purchases and drove through a light rain to their home in South Minneapolis.

"So tell me, were you bored at all? Did you find things to do while you were there?" Lucia's mother asked.

In response, Leo almost drove off the road, and both he and Lucia started to laugh.

"Ohmygosh Mom, you have no idea. We'll tell you everything, but first let's just get home. I promise, *I'll make you a special!*" Leo and Lucia laughed again so hard the car almost went off the road a second time.

They arrived home and soon had the car unpacked. Lucia brought Bátor into the house and opened his cage.

"Come on out, Bátor, we're home," she said to her little friend.

But he refused to come out, staying back in the corner of the large, house-like cage.

"Come on, there's nothing to be afraid of," but the cat refused to move.

"Maybe if I take him up to my room he might come out," Lucia said. "Maybe he just needs to be alone for a while."

She took the cage up to her room. "Come on little kitty. You don't have to be afraid."

Bátor looked through the slats and saw they were alone. He padded out of the cage and over to Lucia to rub his face against her leg.

"See? You don't have to be afraid."

The cat seemed to assess her room then proceeded to rub himself against her leg a few more times and returned once more to his cage and meowed. Just then Lucia heard a click and the sound of a sliding wood panel. Bátor came back out of the cage.

Sitting on his back with a scruff of fur in each hand was Aranck.

221

Lucia gasped for air. A Lytle was in her South Minneapolis bedroom.

"Ohmygosh, Aranck, what are you doing here?" she whispered. "Are … are you in trouble? Does your family know you're here?"

"I'm not in trouble, Lucia Boyd. They don't know where I am exactly, but they know I am with you."

"But why are you here? Why leave Lylian? Why leave The Tilt?"

"It is time for us to learn more about the rest of the world. So they can learn more about us. We were almost destroyed as a race. And few outside of Lylian would ever have known of us. It is time for Lytles to stand up and be counted in the world."

"But why come here?" she asked. "Why me? Why trust me?"

"Because you and your father showed us great courage and caring," the Mek said. " I chose you because I believe in you."

Lucia stared at the little visitor for a few minutes.

"Well, let's go downstairs," she said. "I think we better tell my parental units the adventure isn't over."

Lylian, Lost Land of the Lytles, is the
debut novel of **Thom Sandberg**,
loosely based on the Lake Harriet Elf
(www.mrlittleguy.com). He is a long-time
advertising creative, having worked in
Minneapolis, London, Istanbul and Tokyo.
He lives in Minneapolis with his wife,
daughter and two cats.